Tales Out Of School

Tales Out Of School

Owen Kelly

Blackstaff Press

British Library Cataloguing in Publication Data

Kelly, Owen
  Tales out of school.
  1. Northern Ireland — Fiction
  I. Title
  823'.9'1FS   PR6061.E49/

ISBN 0-85640-199-4

Published by Blackstaff Press Limited, 3 Galway Park, Dundonald,
Belfast, BT16 0AN, with the assistance of the Arts Council of
Northern Ireland.

ISBN 0 85640 199 4

Printed and bound in Great Britain by Billing and Sons Limited,
Guildford, London, Oxford, Worcester.

Contents

One Horse Town Revisited

I went back to the old place recently to bury Donovan. Not personally, you understand. There was an undertaker to take care of the actual work, and a clergyman who spoke of one of nature's gentlemen in a I-hope-you've-gone-where-I-suspect-you-haven't tone. But it was the demise of Donovan that had me standing in a little sloping cemetery on the slopes of the Sperrins, and there was water in the bottom of the grave.

'He wouldn't like that,' said Hegarty, nudging me and nodding at the water. For cooking and for washing, Donovan intoned to me once, water is grand stuff. But for drinking, God, man it could kill you.

Donovan was the friend and mentor of my early teaching days. He was not a teacher. He described himself as a part-time layabout, which was in a sense true, for he spent eight months of the year building England's motorways, thus accumulating enough cash to spend the other four carousing at home. He was in fact the kind of man that men take to at once and women warn their daughters against. I met him on the day I was appointed to the local school, which was the same day that a horse dropped dead in the local forge. There is, I hope, no sinister connection between all these events.

I had been incautious enough while in my cups on graduation night to tell a couple of fellow students that I had been offered a job in the village, and when they pressed me for details I had described it as a one-horse town. The death of the horse made headlines in the local paper and some days later a telegram arrived at the school enquiring what I would do now that the horse was dead. The authors were the same pair of rascally students, but the departure of the horse, whatever significance it might have had for me, had been well and truly over-shadowed by another, more awesome experience. I had met the clerical manager.

The clerical manager was an imposing man who lived in a suitably imposing residence at the lower end of the village. As I trudged up the steps and rang the bell, the horse was being winched out of the forge, to the embarrassment of the blacksmith, the chagrin of the owner and the huge delight of the local population. The manager, a sunbathing dog and myself must have been the only living creatures not super-vising the exit of the horse.

The manager opened the door and without deigning me a word, turned on his heel and stalked into his study. I followed, somewhat diffidently, for I was none too sure how to handle a situation like this. Did one stand at the door and complete the formalities there? Should I have gone to the tradesman's entrance? Was there a tradesman's entrance? These questions, plus the smell of furniture polish, old books and sanctity were still perplexing me when he spoke again.

'Come in,' he said, eyeing me coldly. He did not ask me to sit, though there were plenty of chairs. I stood guiltily in front of the desk and he leaned back in his chair, staring through me at some distant corner of his domain. I didn't know what I was feeling guilty about, but I felt sure he would find something.

'Where were you for the past two months?' he suddenly demanded, and I realised instantly that while the laws of physics demand that everybody be somewhere, wherever I was would turn out to be the wrong place. The uninitiated might be forgiven for thinking that this was a run-of-the-mill type of question, standard interview stuff, but it was not. Appointments in village schools always came wrapped up with strings, in the form of extracurricular activities irreverently known among the rural teaching fraternity as po-jerking. No doubt the local veterans had heard of a prospective new appointment and had cunningly skived off to their favourite watering-places, leaving no one to mind the shop. The same grapevine that had alerted them had alerted me and I had hightailed it to Wales, there to dig numerous holes in the unoffending landscape at the behest of one George Wimpey, whose name is held by some to mean We Import More

2

Paddies Every Year. While I was engaged in this lucrative pursuit, there was no one to organise whatever had to be organised by the local junior teacher.

'I've been in Wales,' I confessed, but forebore to hold up my calloused hands in proof. Old George was a reasonably indulgent employer and I had no callouses to show.

'Wales!' he yelped. 'Wales!' I half expected him to add, in the manner of George the Third, 'Pray, Sir, where is Wales?' but he didn't. He merely sat and viewed me with distaste. I recognised the disease right away, a bad case of the parish-pump syndrome. Anywhere beyond the county boundary was heathen country where the natives practised cannibalism, went with girls and probably drank beer as well. On this last point I was right on target.

'Where's your Pioneer Pin?' he demanded, glowering at the lapel of my jacket for evidence that I was a member of that dedicated teetotal fraternity. Having always had a quiet conviction that a jar or two, like work, was a grand thing in moderation, I now realised that an aspiring young schoolmaster ought to publicly advertise his aversion to drink.

'I lost it,' I lied cheerfully, but to my surprise this barefaced hypocrisy drew no reply.

'There were a few things you could have been doing,' he informed me icily. 'I was looking for you, but no one seemed to know where you were.'

This was not quite true. A lot of people knew where I was, including my devious schoolmaster brother, already teaching in a nearby village, but then he owed me a few quid and the least hint of my whereabouts, he knew, would have probably resulted in my calling in the debt prematurely. The others who knew kept silent for reasons that would no doubt unfold.

I muttered a few platitudes about travel broadening the mind, and the need for a few bob to tide me over until the Minister of Education parted reluctantly with the first salary cheque. He listened indifferently to my babbled explanation for a while, then dismissed it all with a wave of his hand.

'I'm offering you a job,' he said, managing to convey considerable distaste and a strong desire to have second thoughts. He picked up his phone and dialled a number. A tiny disembodied voice squeaked in the earpiece.

'Come down here, I want you a minute,' he growled into the receiver without bothering to identify himself. Many subsequent experiences were to assure me that no form of identification was ever required. We waited in silence for the arrival of the minion.

'What were you doing in Wales?' he demanded, after a silence that seemed to have lasted for a week and a half. Mercifully his indifferent attention to my babbled narrative was interrupted by the doorbell. He got up and ushered in a small, nervous man in sports jacket and flannels. The newcomer approached us hesitantly, halted diffidently at the desk and stood shifting his weight from one foot to the other. His upper lip kept moving back and forth in what I supposed was a desire to grin. The manager made no effort to introduce him, or even acknowledge his existence, but I eventually gathered that he was the principal of one of the half-dozen or so schools scattered about the place. The lesson was clear enough. If the manager didn't take principals under his notice then assistant teachers with the ink still wet on their diplomas counted for a lot less. The newcomer's fidgetting, I was soon to discover, was a characteristic of his breed and class.

'I want you to witness this,' growled the manager, and for a terrifying minute I felt sure I was to be the victim of some barbaric rite of initiation they hadn't warned us about in college. But he merely shoved a pen and paper across the desk at the newcomer and bade him sign it. He did this, and winked at me.

'Is that all?' asked the witness, but he got no reply, so he left, backing away from the presence in the manner of an Oriental slave. Only the salaam was missing.

The manager then thrust the paper at me.

'This is your contract,' he informed me. 'Sign it.'

I duly signed and shuffled towards the door, doing a passable impersonation of the departed headmaster. The manager followed me to the top of the steps where he delivered the final comment of the interview.

'You're signed, sealed and delivered,' he told me, with all the satisfaction of a man who has his enemy where he wants him. 'So now you'll do as you're bid.'

Before I could compose a suitably outraged reply, he had stepped back inside, leaving the August street to the sunbathing dog and myself. The dog got up and wagged his tail and both of us strolled companionably up the street as far as the local bar. The dog paused to wash some dust from the hubcap of a battered Rover and I stepped into the pub's cool creaky interior. There was only one customer in the place, a cheerful looking fellow in his thirties. He was of muscular build, clad in jeans and a lumberjack shirt, and somewhat unusually, for such adornment was rare in those days, he had a reddish beard. He was carefully supervising the pouring of a bottle of stout.

'On the thumb, young Tommy,' he was exhorting the youthful

4

barman. 'On the thumb.' '

'I'm always tellin' these young fellas that the only way to pour a bottle of stout,' he announced to me, by way of making me welcome, 'is to put the thumb against the glass, like this,' he demonstrated, 'and pour the stout like so,' he demonstrated again. 'It's an art, ye know,' he told me seriously. 'It's not a bad evening', Master.'

The demise of the horse had not, apparently, monopolised all the resources of the bush telegraph, for all male teachers in rural Ulster were known as Master, to their faces at any rate, and I felt a certain pride at being identified as one of the brotherhood.

'Ye were up with His Nibs,' he continued, 'I seen ye goin' up the steps.'

'I was,' I agreed.

'Hard man to talk to, His Nibs,' he said, taking a reflective pull from the glass. 'My name's Donovan.'

I introduced myself.

'What's your first name?' I asked.

'Donovan,' he told me, with a huge grin. 'What'll ye take?'

Refreshments were duly purchased and we wished each other luck.

'Ye're married, Master?' Donovan queried.

I denied this and levelled the accusation at Donovan. He gazed thoughtfully into his glass.

'I don't rightly know,' he said, with a look of great perplexity.

'That's an odd answer, Donovan,' I said.

'Dammit, ye sound like a schoolmaster already,' he laughed. 'Well, it's like this. I did get married once and we went to Bray for the honeymoon. When we got to the hotel she went out to get a paper and I went into the bar for a drink. That's the last I ever seen of her. But sure I had a gran' week of it on me own.' He finished off his drink and stood up. 'Well, anyway, Master, I'm away. See and enjoy yerself. I'll be seein' ye again.'

'Is that yarn true?' I asked the barman as Donovan drove off in the battered Rover.

'Aw, I think there's something to it all right,' said the youth. 'But with Donovan you'd never be rightly sure.'

So I was standing in a sloping cemetery on the slopes of the Sperrins, noting the fact that for a man who had attracted so much hem-snatching disapproval in his lifetime, he had also attracted a lot of friends. Donovan had taken me under his wing and in his freewheeling, philosophical way had counselled and cushioned me against those molehills of difficulty that become mountains to the new and untried country teacher.

5

'Had he a wife?' asked a mourner of me, in a thunderous whisper.

'Damn the wife,' the other replied, somewhat ambiguously. This aggressive statement, however, was merely to emphasise Donovan's *de facto* bachelor status, for they're hot on emphasis in the Sperrins.

It was appropriate that the defender of Donovan's marital status was small, for it was a tenet of his philosophy that there was 'always a wee man'. A wee man that could get you into a pub that never shut but never advertised the fact, a wee man who seldom took a drink himself, but would, just this once, seein' it's yourself that's askin'.

He had an unerring instinct for the 'wee men'. Travelling home from football matches on Sunday afternoons through the deserted villages, Donovan would suddenly stop and accost the only native in sight. There would be a brief exchange of words, a few hearty laughs and we were in for the rest of the evening. Down entries, over walls and behind the solid respectability of the Ulster Sabbath, the wee man would lead us into another world.

He made a mistake only once, and that was by sheer accident. While negotiating with the wee man one Sunday afternoon, a stout lady walking a Peke suddenly materialised and sabotaged the whole transaction. We were some distance away and couldn't hear what was going on, but Donovan was never one to let a situation out of his control. It appeared that the lady was an aggressive teetotaller and she launched into a lecture on the evils of drink. Donovan took it all submissively and blamed his dissipation on a poor upbringing. He swore off it on the spot and she invited him home for tea. Off went Donovan, without a backward glance, and left us foundering in the draughty old Rover.

The lady was delighted with her conversion and she fed him well and introduced him to the family. It then transpired that Donovan, feeling expansive, proceeded to entertain the family to stories, which, if he actually did tell them, would have got him expelled from a stokers' mess.

'Good gracious, Mr Donovan,' the startled lady exclaimed, according to Donovan's version. 'Do you always talk like that?'

'Only when I'm sober, ma'am,' Donovan replied and made his majestic way out.

As I stood at the gate and watched the crowd trickle out, I thought it was civil of Donovan to depart during the school holidays. I knew they'd be eulogising and burying him for another couple of days round the hillsides. I decided to stay for a day or two.

The First Day

The city schools where I did my stints of teaching practice had all opened for business at the civilised hour of half past nine, and it simply never occurred to me that other schools might have other ideas. At a quarter past nine, I set out to walk the half-mile or so to the scene of my future struggle against ignorance and I was nearly halfway there when I noticed a curious absence of children on the road. In fact the only other person on the road was a smallish man with an army surplus kitbag slung over one shoulder. These kitbags were very popular with schoolchildren, for they made durable and cheap schoolbags, and with workers of all types. This particular worker wore turned-down Wellingtons, and a double-vented, tattered sports jacket, known locally, I soon learned, as a bum-flapper. It was only when I fell in step with this personage that I realised he was no labourer hastening to work, merely a biggish schoolboy. He jerked his head in a form of greeting and eyed me suspiciously.

'You're the new master?' he accused me, and sniffed prodigiously. I was somewhat relieved to note that the sniff was not actually a criticism of me but part of a constant and herculean effort to haul a drop on the end of his nose back into the shelter of his nostril. 'They don't have standards now, ye know,' he informed me solemnly. Now I knew even then that people believed that standards of education were falling, that the education children were receiving was inferior to what their parents had received, while the hedge-schoolmasters who had taught their ancestors had imparted a quality of learning unsurpassed in any modern university and all for twopence a week. Even so, such blanket condemnation from such a young consumer startled me.

'Naw,' he went on, 'they call them primaries now. Ye know, primary wan, primary two an' all.'

I was about to mention that I had heard some rumours of this revolutionary change but when I took another sideways look at my informant I decided to enter into the spirit of the thing.

'I'm glad you told me,' I said gratefully, 'I could have made a right fool of myself in here.'

On this comradely note we turned in at the school gate and headed for the front door.

At the door my companion developed a burst of speed, shot down the corridor, kicked off both Wellingtons and disappeared into a classroom in his stockinged feet. The school, I had been warned in advance, was brand new and no one, teacher or pupil, was allowed to wear outdoor shoes inside the building. Sandals or slippers were required, but such niceties did not carry a lot of weight with him. I had omitted to bring spare footwear, so I carefully wiped my shoes on the mat and followed him into what I assumed was the principal's room. I based this assumption on the fact that I could see the principal inside when the boy opened the door.

I was wrong. It was my class and the principal stood at the front with the roll-book under his arm, pointedly studying his watch.

'Andy,' said the principal, pointing at the large boy who was squeezing himself into a desk, 'has been fifteen minutes late for school every day since he first started. We used to start at half past nine and Andy arrived religiously every morning at a quarter to ten. Now that we start at a quarter past nine, he comes at half past. If we started at four in the afternoon, I'm sure he would arrive at a quarter past.'

I got the message. The principal was warning me not to fall into Andy's evil ways. He then turned to the class.

'This is Mr Kelly, your new teacher,' he pointed out somewhat unnecessarily, and added, more to the point, 'See that you do what he tells you.'

There were twenty-eight boys and girls in the class and they focussed their twenty-eight pairs of eyes on me, probing like X-rays for signs of weakness. I had a momentary sense of terror. My previous experiences with classes had always included an experienced teacher ready to quell riots or other forms of mutiny. In a very few moments I was going to be on my own, with no back-up force just out of sight. I longed for a quick translation back to the building site I had recently left.

The principal spent another few minutes briefing me on various points about books, lessons and discipline, then he handed me the roll-book and departed.

I sat at the desk and, having fixed the class with a stony stare proceeded to call out the names. I required, in a very official tone, everyone to stand up as I called their names. This was a futile attempt to learn their names in a hurry. At the end of the exercise I knew only some of them, so I put the register away. The class and I got down to studying each other intently. All we needed, I felt, was a large pot simmering gently in the foreground and we would have a Victorian woodcut of missionary-meets-cannibal-tribe come to life. One wrong move, I knew, and I was for the pot.

In the midst of this frantic mental activity, the door was suddenly thrust open and a bulging postbag entered, mounted on the considerable frontage of the local postman.

'Mornin' Master,' he greeted me. 'Gran' day.'

He then ignored me completely and surveyed the class with a searching eye. Twenty-eight pairs of eyes watched him expectantly.

'Mickey Joe Bradley,' he announced and a little girl with glasses put up her hand. Patently she was not Mickey Joe anybody and in any case I knew she was Doreen Duffy, for had I not marked the register and hers was one of the few faces I could put a name to. The postman made his stately way to her desk and tossed a couple of letters on to it. Then he turned away and the tail of his jacket swept her books to the floor. He swung round to her again and placed his boot firmly on the books.

'Throw this in to Biddy,' he ordered and a packet thudded on to her desk. I watched in fascination as he called out more names and hands were thrust out to receive mail. Then with the round of the classroom completed he stalked out without a further word.

'What was all that about?' I asked in awe. I was wondering just how a raw recruit straight from college could possibly follow this performance.

'Please Sir,' chorussed the class, 'we deliver the letters. It saves him the bother.'

Of course. What else. It was just a normal social service provided by the school.

'Well, shut the door, somebody,' I said, for the postman had omitted this trifling nicety, but as a horde of willing hands rushed to do this a distraught female burst into the room. She was, as near as I could judge from my cowering position behind the desk, about seven feet tall and built like an oak tree. I frantically examined my conscience as she bore down on me ferociously. I hadn't even been an hour in the place. How could I have incurred the wrath of a total stranger in that time?

She skidded to a halt before me, thrust two hands the size of shovels down on my desk and wheezed. The class watched with interest.

'Come on quick, Master,' she gasped, seizing my arm in an iron grip. 'Come on quick, the cow's calvin'.'

Before I could collect my scattered wits we were travelling at a half-gallop down the road and into her farmyard. As we travelled she explained that the menfolk were at the fair and it was just them to be gallivantin' to fairs when there was work to be done and what would the eedjits do without weemin anyway. There was more in this vein, but I paid little heed to it, for I was taking off my jacket and frantically trying to recall what I had seen farmers do in similar circumstances when I was a child. She careered off and came charging back with a wicked-looking pair of scissors, a bottle of iodine and other paraphernalia for the occasion.

Fortunately the birth, as is usual in these cases, for cows are well-organised animals, was totally uncomplicated and in no time at all I was able to tell the lady that the cow had become the mother of a fine bouncing beast of uncertain weight and wobbly legs.

'God bless ye, Master,' she said gratefully and whipped from her capacious apron pocket a bottle of stout and an opener. 'Now you jist stan' there an' drink that for you're the boy disarves it.'

She was between me and the door so I stood and consumed her hospitality. As I drank, I considered many things. What, for example, would the principal say when he discovered that I was not at my post? What would the Ministry of Education think of their newest employee standing ankle-deep in clabber and drinking stout on a fine September morning. I also formulated some opinions on the shortcomings of the training college syllabus.

'I'm terrible sorry about yer new shoot an' yalla shoes,' she said apologetically, making ineffectual swipes at me with a wisp of hay. But the suit was far from new and despite their polish the shoes were ancient, so I strolled back to the school with a deep sense of achievement.

The principal merely smiled. A veteran of thirty-five years of country schoolmastering, he took the practice of veterinary midwifery by his staff in his stride. The class, no strangers to farmyard smells, greeted me with respectful grins. With the aid of an obliging cow whose sense of timing was nothing short of miraculous, I had started off on the right foot. An elderly suit and well-worn shoes was a small price to pay. It seemed entirely fitting then that my first, if somewhat belated, official lesson should be on the art and inner mystery of multiplication.

Taken to the Fair

At five past three on the Friday of my first week's teaching Donovan thrust his grinning, hairy face round the door of the empty classroom.

'Boys-a-dear,' he said, shaking his head in wonder. 'You schoolmasters have the quare times of it. Five past three an' quet already!'

He strolled around the empty room, whistling between his teeth.

'Tell ye what,' he announced. 'It's the fair day. How about goin' for the crack? If ye're goin' to tache in the country, ye'll want to see how the natives operate.'

'Donovan,' I said, 'that's a sound educational idea.'

'Educational. The very word,' said Donovan, as if he had never heard of it before. I was beginning to realise that Donovan was anything but the ignoramus he pretended to be.

'I never took much notice of education meself,' he told me as we got into the car. 'The only thing I wanted to do was to be able to put me hand in me hip pocket and hold meself out at arm's length. It's true. An oul' uncle, half-cracked he was, he made me believe when I was a nipper that I could do it. Begod, I practised for a while, but I giv it up when I broke me wrist. The mother giv me a quare skelpin', I'm tellin' ye and she wudn't let the uncle across the door for a twelve-month when she foun' out what happened. Wanes'll believe

12

anythin' if ye tell them the right way.'

I recalled the story of Donovan's honeymoon and kept silent. As we travelled the four miles into the village, Donovan pointed out various houses to me and regaled me with hilarious accounts of their occupiers and their eccentricities.

'Over there's Barney Duggan's. He used to make poteen. The police knew he was at it and boys they waited months to get him. Begod, one fine day they got the boul' Barney up at the Gap, boilin' away like a good 'un. Well, they carted Barney an' the poteen an' the still away to the barracks an' they emptied the poteen down the sink. That's what they do, ye know, empty it down the sink. They put the still out in the yard, an' they filled up all the papers and toul' Barney he was for the high jump at the next sessions. Begod, Barney was no dozer. He went back in the middle of the night, over the barrack wall, and made off with the still. He got it roun' the back road to Johnny's hayshed and buried it in the hay. They sarched the country high an' low but they foun' no still. Jizby, the D.I. was hoppin' mad when he heard about it, but sure they had to drop the case. No evidence, ye see.'

He was about to tell me how Coul' Trousers earned his curious nickname, but by this time we were in the village and the fair was all around us. Now the fair was no piped music and sideshows job. It was the monthly confrontation between the farmers and the cattle-dealers, those burly men of another time, with rolled-up trousers, brown boots, ashplants and wads of notes. I soon learned that an encounter between a dalin' man and a farmer was something no sideshow could have competed with.

'Wait till ye see this,' said Donovan gleefully, as we edged our way into a circle of bystanders, just as the dalin' man approached the beast, with a look of contempt on his face. He walked away a few yards, sneering, then he came back and took an amused look at the farmer's impassive face. Then he walked away again, and just before he was out of earshot, he fired a query over his shoulder.

'Whaddya want for it?'

He didn't deign to refer to the animal by species, preferring to suggest that it was some form of worthless mutation and he was only asking out of courtesy. The farmer mentioned a price that seemed to bring the dealer to the verge of a stroke. He stood rooted to the spot, poking at his ear with a stubby, nicotined finger. This was to indicate that the oul' ear trouble was at him again, that he couldn't be sure that he had heard what he thought he had heard. If he was interested, he announced, he would offer half the amount, for the baste would be dear enough at that.

The offer produced in the farmer alternating bouts of laughter and obscenity as temperament and religious conviction struggled for control. The bystanders stood in stoical detachment, performing a sort of ritual dance consisting of shifting weight from one foot to the other and tapping the boots gently together.

The dealer then approached the animal and studied it again. He managed to convey the impression, to me at any rate, that he was only doing this out of curiosity because he had never seen a creature like it before, didn't expect to again and wanted to enlarge his experience of animal freaks before this one dropped dead on the street.

'Tell ye what I'll do,' he said tentatively, beginning to edge away. 'I'll give ye forty poun'.'

'Sixty!' the owner snarled, spitting on the ground.

'Name-a-God,' screamed the dealer, pop-eyed with shock. But then the haggling commenced and bit by bit they edged nearer to agreement, nearer to the real figure the farmer had in mind. There was still a gap, of course, but Donovan nudged me and stepped into it.

'What's between ye, boys?' he asked, somewhat superfluously, for we all knew the simple arithemetic involved. The dealer and the owner ignored him, but the information was delivered deadpan by a bystander.

'Split it,' ordered Donovan, grabbing a hand of each party and endeavouring to make them slap their palms together, the outward and visible sign of agreement. Some resistance, punctuated with spitting and swearing then ensued, and a price was agreed — an amount within a pound of what the owner wanted — and the dealer was apparently willing to pay. Since payment was made in a nearby pub and the difference several times over might well be consumed on the premises, it all seemed a waste of time. It was, Donovan assured me, a necessary part of my education.

We trooped into the pub on the heels of the farmer, the dealer and their retinues. It was a big place, which was just as well, for two carloads of sheepfarmers from North Derry and Plumbridge were barrelling their way in as we arrived. It wasn't a sheep fair, so this was a day out for these redfaced men in heavy sweaters, as they exchanged genial insults and called for bottles of stout. The air was thick with smoke and conversation.

One man was complaining to another about the shortcomings of a dog.

'He's not worth a damn, I'm tellin' ye, he couldn't turn roun' without fallin'.'

14

'Sure ye could cure that wi' a wee bitta lead in his ear.'

'How the hell wud ye put lead in a dog's ear?'

'With a gun.'

'Heh, with a gun — jizby that's a good un!'

Another man was telling how his bike had been stolen from outside a dance-hall, six years before. Brand new it had been, he assured his listeners, only it had a faulty dynamo.

'I was on the other side of Maghera the other night an' I near driv over a fella trying to fix his headlamp. I got out to give him a han' and sure as I'm here, it was my bike. There was the same bit of a cigarette packet folded under the spring inside the headlamp. I knew it was mine all right, for I wrote a couple of messages on the same bit of a packet the day before the bike was stole.'

'What did ye do?' asked one of the company.

'Do? I done nothin'. Sure what wud I do? There was me, drivin' a good motor, bought an' paid for, and thon thievin' bugger was still ridin' a stolen bike.'

'If it wus me, I'da kicked his bloody...ah, begod here's Donovan.'

We were welcomed into the company like long-lost travellers and everybody enquired after everybody else's relations, family, in-laws and outlaws. In a corner of the room someone was mangling 'Slieve Gallion's Braes' in a gravelly voice.

'Somebody in here's not well,' remarked Donovan and the company's dutiful laugh was interrupted by a threat from among the smoke. 'Quiet when me da's singin',' the voice ordered.

'Right ye are, Joe,' said Donovan, winking genially all round.

Over by the fireplace, a tipsy gent aroused himself from slumber and sleepily eyed the company. He wiped his face with the elaborate care of the truly plastered and with immense effort removed a crumpled packet of cigarettes from his jacket pocket. With considerable difficulty he lit the tipped end, inhaled deeply and threw the cigarette away. 'Them cigarettes is rotten,' he told the fire, and dozed off again.

We wandered off again through the fair. Donovan accosted a passing citizen and asked him if he had seen Big John.

'Ah, he's not here the day. He buried the uncle yesterday,' the man replied.

'Aye, did he?' Donovan asked with interest. 'Was he dead?'

'Aye.'

'Well,' said Donovan profoundly, 'there wasn't much else he could do with him, then.'

We wandered on and joined a group round a stall where a

gypsy-looking character was selling hardware. He was extolling the virtues of his wares with total disregard for truth.

'These pliers,' he announced, 'are made from the finest German surgical steel. They'll cut anything. Look,' and he made a ferocious attack on a length of wire.

'Gran' for pullin' teeth,' remarked Donovan, 'but a bit fancy for balin' wire.'

The dealer glared, for he had a monopoly on wisecracks, but Donovan grinned disarmingly and as we moved on the pliers were miraculously transmuted to Sheffield steel. Further along the street we met a small, foxy-looking individual with a menacing squint.

'How are ye, Fred?' enquired Donovan solicitously. 'This is the new schoolmaster out at Drumneeny.'

Fred glared at me suspiciously.

'How about a climb up the Eagle's Rock the morra, Fred?' Donovan said. 'We'll show this fella the view from the top of it.'

'No fear,' said Fred. 'It'll be a wet day. The last time I went up the mountain with you, Donovan, I got a founder and lay in bed for a week.'

'That's no fun on your own, right enough,' Donovan commiserated. 'Who said the weather would be bad?' he went on. subtly implying that he had made his own arrangements about the weather.

'It was on the wireless this morning.'

'The wireless,' howled Donovan derisively. 'Likely wan of them chape Japanese things ye bought from that gypsy. Sure what would they know about the weather? Ye couldn't heed them.'

Fred was adamant that he was climbing no Eagle's Rock, so we left him.

'Me granny,' said Donovan, 'has more spunk in her and she's ten years dead. Mind you, he knows every inch of the mountain but he jist takes these thrawn notions and ye cudn't shift him. He's a mane twister, too, so make sure ye never lend him money. Ye'll never get it back, or if ye do get it off him, and ye'd need a spanner, I'll guarantee ye there'll be bits of skin stuck to it.'

The fair was thinning out and a chill wind was blowing down the main street. In spite of Donovan, I thought maybe the Japanese transistor might be right. He stood with his thumbs in his belt morosely surveying the street up and down.

'There's no crack at all the day,' he said mournfully. 'Sometimes I wonder why I bother to come home at all?'

'Then why do you?' I asked.

'Fellas like me are important in a place like this,' grinned Donovan. 'Sure if we weren't about, these gobshites would have nobody to look down on.'

Another drink seemed to be called for, so we went into yet another pub and ordered. The door flew open and what appeared to be a deranged dwarf hurtled across the floor waving fists the size of golf-balls and screaming falsetto threats round a single tooth that conveyed hilarity rather than menace.

'I'm goney bate the head aff ye, Donovan!' he yelled dancing up and down, to the vast amusement of the customers. The little man was definitely under the influence.

'It was you, ye hairy bugger ye,' he shouted and Donovan languidly stretched out a huge hand and placed it against the wee man's diminutive chest.

His miniature fists thrashed the air.

'It wasn't me,' Donovan said soothingly, smothering a laugh.

'It was so,' screamed the wee man. 'She said it was a hairy fella and there's nobody else about here as hairy as you.'

'She was mistaken,' soothed Donovan. 'Here, have a sup of that,' and he thrust his glass into the other's hands.

With the wee man thus occupied we made our exit amid howls of amusement. Outside, Donovan collapsed on to the pub window-sill and shook with laughter.

'Tell me,' I asked patiently, 'who or what was that?'

'Och, that's wee Matt,' Donovan explained. 'Pension age if he's a day, and a desperate man for the weemin. Begod I wish I knew how he does it.'

I waited. I was anxious to know exactly how Donovan had posed a threat to mini-Matt's love life.

'I was dandering up the Brae Road the other night,' Donovan went on, amid hysterical sobs of laughter, 'an' I foun' yer man lyin' face down on the verge. I was sure he was dead. I picked him up by the scruff of his neck an' the slack of his trousers, an' here, boys, he let a screech outta him would waken the dead. An' well he might screech,' — a look of recollected wonder crossed Donovan's face — 'for there was a lassie under him. Her legs were shinin' in the moonlight like the shafts of a barra.'

I joined him on the window sill. 'Well, go on, what happened then?' I asked, during a pause in the laughter.

'I ran for me life,' sobbed Donovan. 'Sure I had to. Thon lassie's tongue would have flayed a donkey. I never heard language the like of it,' he ended piously.

17

'But why,' I asked, 'did he not recognise you there and then?'

Donovan looked at me pityingly.

'He had his eyes shut,' he explained patiently. 'He was hurted, don't ye see. It's boun' to be a sore thing, bein' interrupted like that.'

I got the message and sat for a while in near-quiet contemplation of the scene. The spectacle of Donovan holding the little man up in the air while a prone, semi-naked and anonymous female read him chapter and verse of his ancestry was almost too hilarious to think about.

Donovan stood up.

'Come on,' he said. 'We'll go and get ourselves a fry or so. Then we'll get squared up and go to the dance in the Castle. We should be all right there. If scruffy wee divils like Matt can get weemin, a couple of presentable fellas like us should be able to manage it too.'

As we dandered back to the car, Donovan was apologetic.

'Dammit there was no crack through the fair at all the day. Ah, but sure the morra's another day.'

I wondered exactly what Donovan meant by crack. If dalin' men who could have been on the stage, cynical sheepmen offering to cure off-balance dogs by putting lead in their ears, sellers of surgical pliers and demented dwarfs tackling men three times their size in defence of their honour didn't constitute a fair bit of crack and a certain amount of enlightenment, the rest of the evening could hardly be quiet.

Rural Mafia

In the days when the railways meandered across the countryside, the village had been at the end of the line. The bus-line also ended there. Clearly, the chiefs of the great transport undertakings had marked the mountains to the north of the place with the legend *'Here be dragons,'* and left the natives to their own devices.

Five hundred people, give or take a couple, lived there, and a somewhat lesser number of dogs. It had eleven pubs, enough to make sure no one went thirsty. There were three churches to take care of the spiritual welfare of those who needed it, which was everybody. There had once been a temperance hotel, but with eleven pubs glaring at it from all corners, it soon gave up the ghost. There was another establishment loosely called a hotel, presided over by an elderly female, but there was no historic evidence that anyone ever stayed there.

It had the usual variety of shops, including two with no visible stock or identifiable customers. In these two establishments bands of local characters gathered to swap yarns and tell each other lies, particularly on Saturday nights. These levees were patronised by the local tee-totalers, a small enough band, and those who had no money for drink, a larger and more interesting group entirely.

Its society, like Gaul, was divided into three parts; the haves, the

19

have-nots and the couldn't-care-less. The have-nots desperately wanted to have, but would have died sooner than admit it. The haves were vigorously determined that the have-nots should not get above themselves. The couldn't-care-less were loftily indifferent to the pretensions of both sides. You could always tell a have from a have-not by their conversation. The haves called the place a town. The have-nots, in colourful and censorable invective, described it as something entirely different.

On one issue all sides were united, albeit in a very loose and unreliable alliance, and that was the matter of The Mountainy Men. These were the hill farmers, mostly sheepmen, burly weatherbeaten characters who ranged their hills from dawn to dusk in all weathers. They had no time for men who stopped work at six o'clock and had indoor plumbing. They did, however, have wives and the wives had large, bulging handbags, stuffed with turkey money, egg money and the profits from the sale of pet pigs. They were also non-drivers to the last woman.

The haves cast envious eyes on those bulging handbags and dusted off their maps. A delegation from the local business community duly waited on the manager of the bus company and showed the wonders of their world to him. He was impressed, and in due course a bus, laden with dignitaries from the worlds of transport and business, nosed its hesitant way into the surrounding mountains.

Now on the other side of the mountain dwelt Big Joe. He couldn't read a map but he could read signs, particularly pound signs. He owned two decrepit taxis, and a lorry held together with baling wire. A simple soul, he reasoned if anybody was going anywhere he was bringing them, usually to another village where he and his relations had business interests.

When the trial bus slowly edged its way round a narrow corner of the mountain road, Big Joe's lorry was parked there. There was no way the bus could pass the lorry. As the transport experts exchanged significant glances, Big Joe, his face covered with grease and sweaty innocence, appeared from the front of the lorry. He waved his hands helplessly. The oul' lorry, ye see. Broke down. He wondered, would maybe two or three of them get aff the bus and give him a wee push. He was tarrible sorry for the trouble, and would they min' their good clothes, and that's it, all together, lads. As he drove off in a cloud of black smoke, the cherished hopes of an extended busline disappeared with him.

If you can't beat them, hire them, reasoned the business men and on the next fair day Big Joe's do-it-yourself transport fleet ferried the womenfolk into the village.

It would be appropriate now to mention a local custom. It was a fiction of rural life that farmers had no time to go shopping for themselves. For a race of men who claimed to wear the trousers they were suprisingly complacent about who actually selected them.

If a farmer needed a pair of shoes or a shirt, his wife would go into the village and bring home several items. It might look as if she was offering him a choice but this was not the case. She needed the assistance of her dungaree-clad model to make up her mind. After the selection was made, the rejected items were brought back to the shop and the item kept was then, and not till then, paid for. It was on this precise point that Big Joe and his wily relations sabotaged the great transport undertaking. They brought, in the process, joy to the have-nots, red faces to the haves and cries of I-told-you-so from the couldn't-care-less group. In the process, of course, Joe and company redirected the egg money to its rightful destination, their own pockets.

As the first wave of strangers hit the street, one made straight for the shoe shop. The shop was owned by the man who was the brains behind the transport scheme, and he was more than a little uneasy when the lady announced that she was looking for a pair of shoes for her husband. A local could have brought the shoes home, made her selection and returned the unwanted ones. This stranger wouldn't be back until the next fair day. Worse, she might never come back.

The lady was a mind-reader.

'I know what ye're thinkin', Mr Brown,' she announced candidly. 'Ye're thinkin' I cud walk out that door with six pairs of shoes and you'd never see me or them again.'

Mr Brown made deprecating noises and gestures, apologising to the lady for her blunt, if accurate perception.

'I'll tell what I'll do,' said the lady magnanimously. 'I'll take away only the left shoe of each pair. And when I bring them back, I'll take two pairs instead of one.'

Mr Brown brightened at this. He spoke sympathetically of the weather, learnedly of the world situation and hopefully for the turf-cutting prospects as he parcelled up six left shoes and saw the lady off the premises.

He never did see her again. Many fairs were to elapse before he found out that her husband, by this time deceased, had only one leg. The left one.

Another keen supporter of the transport enterprise was the local tobacconist. He was, according to the haves, a man who loved an intelligent conversation. The have-nots called him a gossip. Either way, his shop was often crowded, especially on a fair day, with his less industrious cronies. On this fair day a stranger walked in and asked for ten Blues. The tobacconist was engrossed in the yarn he was telling and he served his customer absent-mindedly. He swept the two-shilling piece into the drawer, dropped the cigarettes and three pence change on the counter with a flamboyant gesture and never, as the quaint local phrase had it, broke his discourse.

The man had been gone some time before the alarm bells rang in the tobacconist's head. He yanked the cash register open and sure enough, the coin was foreign.

'I'll get him,' he roared. 'Bloody mountain man, thinks he can walk in here and take me on like that. I'll fix him. Just you wait.'

'How will ye do that?' one of the company asked, winking round the group, for they were not all friends.

'I know his sort,' snarled the shopkeeper. 'He thinks he's got away with it. He'll be back. He'll try it again.'

'Ach, blethers,' somebody mumbled.

The shopkeeper was right. The man returned, just before the taxi-fleet pulled out. This time he put a pound on the counter and asked for ten Blues. Exchanging knowing grins with his audience, he served his customer and handed over the change, in which he had cunningly included the foreign coin.

The stranger carefully checked his change and the company waited expectantly. He picked out the foreign coin and examined it closely.

'Is this coin legal tender?' he asked eventually, placing it on the counter. The company waited in joyous anticipation.

'Oh, aye, surely,' the shopkeeper assured him.

'Well,' said the man impassively, pushing the coin across the counter with a stubby forefinger. 'Givvis another ten Blues.'

The taxi fleet made only the one trip. The whole truth of the day's rascality never really came to light. Of course, the foreign coin story made the rounds early and lost little in the telling and bit by bit, other pieces of information came to light over the next few months, but little of substance, for the haves were a tight-lipped bunch.

By one of those coincidences that can only happen in real life, a local stumbled on the story of the shoes. It was long, long after the episode of the taxi fleet, and he had to attend a funeral in Tyrone. While standing in the cemetery he overheard a woman telling her companion how she had kept her one-legged, lately departed husband in shoes for nothing for the latter end of his days. Naturally he spread it around when he got back that evening, and that night the pubs were crowded with have-nots, regaling each other with that story, the

22

others they had heard and the far more numerous and ingenious ones they had invented.

'Wud ye luk them!' they crowed. 'Tracks worn to church and chapel and lumps chowed outta the altar rails, and all the time they were trying to fleece the wee mountain men. Listen here boys, ye have to get up early in the mornin' to get the betther of the mountainy men!'

As they winked and hiccoughed their joyous way home, the haves were left in no doubt about one thing. The have-nots were clearly disappointed that the one-legged men was not a human centipede.

The Play's the Thing

'Let me give you a word or three of advice,' said Gerry Johnson to me one bright Saturday morning. He was a principal with twenty years service behind him, so I assumed a posture of profound attention on his garden wall. He laid down his hedge clippers and squatted tailor-fashion on the lawn.

'You will be called on to write references from time to time,' he told me. 'That's no problem in most cases but there'll be the odd occasion when you will be asked to vouch for the sterling qualities of a rank villain. You can't very well refuse, not in a community like this.'

I hadn't thought much about the writing of references but I could see the point he was making.

'Well, what do you do in a case like that?' I asked in some alarm.

'Praise the family,' said Gerry. 'When the lad or lassie is a decent sort, you say so with enthusiasm. If they're rascals, praise the family. Mention what fine hard-working people they are, preferably at some length, but avoid as far as possible any mention of the candidate. The prospective employer will get the message, you'll have done your part and the parents will be delighted with your high opinion of them.'

I admired this piece of practical pyschology and said so. He looked at me with one eye half-shut and head on side.

24

'Psychology,' he informed me gravely, 'is no substitue for horse-sense. Tell me, how would you define an educated person?'

I hastily recalled many discussions on this topic at college.

'I suppose,' I said tentatively, 'an educated person in someone who is aware of how little he knows.'

'You know that, and I know that,' he laughed. 'It's a closely guarded trade secret, best kept from the public. But as far as the majority of the folk around here are concerned, we, for example, are educated men. So we are asked to fill up forms of all types, generally in relation to money. Subsidies, income tax, that sort of thing.'

'Why on earth,' I asked in fright, 'should I be asked to fill up an income tax form? I don't even understand my own yet.'

'The average gent,' said Gerry, 'who asks you to fill up an income tax form for him is well able to do it for himself. Besides, he doesn't want anyone to know anything about his financial affairs, least of all you or me. But to his way of thinking, it's a good way to try out the yarn for size. If you write down what he tells you without batting an eyelid, and why, between ourselves, should you bat an eyelid, for you don't know the right or wrong of it, he reckons the civil servant who reads it will swallow it too. A civil servant and a schoolmaster, they're both educated. Fool one, fool both.'

Not for the first time, and certainly not for the last, it was brought home to me how inadequate my three year's training had been. Not only did most of the theories flop miserably in the classroom, but I was totally unprepared for life outside it.

'I think I'll refer all form-filling to you,' I said resignedly.

'Not at all,' grinned Gerry. 'Assume an inscrutable look and fill away like mad. The fee is paid in cigarettes or Christmas turkeys. Besides you won't be called on all that often for this sort of activity. There's many another form of activity to complicate your life.'

'Don't tell me any more,' I begged.

'I'm about to offer you my most valuable piece of advice,' said Gerry, ignoring my look of misery. 'The world is full of do-gooders, in my experience, and their most fervent wish is to involve people like us in their schemes. For purely selfish reasons, you understand. Now don't get me wrong. Good works are grand things, provided they do some good and are actually done by the do-gooders. In places like this it doesn't work out like that. You will find, before you're very much older, that various people will sidle up to you and ask you to undertake various projects, buckshee of course. You will do the work, they will get the kudos. My own approach is always the same. When anyone slithers up to me and invites me to do something that will

25

interfere with my golf or fishing, unless I actually agree with their objective, I look them straight in the eye and ask "Why?"'

'That seems a reasonable sort of thing to ask,' I commented and he gave me another one-eyed look.

'There is no word in the English language,' he went on, 'that is so disconcerting as "Why?". It puts people on the defensive right away. They have to justify, in reasonably convincing terms, the fact that they want you to do the work while they get the credit. The real truth of course is that your average local reckons that teachers are underworked, overpaid and polish their shoes out of sheer cussedness. They reckon that with all that time on their hands, teachers should organise all the voluntary activities while they get on with the more important things like making money.'

He stood up and lifted his hedge-clippers to show the lesson was over.

'So remember, laddie,' he called after me, 'ask them "Why?" and watch them squirm.'

He was right about one thing. I was exactly two days older when someone did sidle up to me and request my voluntary assistance, but I discovered that there was a world of difference between being a few wet days out of college and being Gerry Johnston. My 'Why?' was met with a brazen 'Because'. On Monday afternoon as I sauntered home from school, a local businessman cruised up alongside and offered me a lift. I should have been suspicious. The sun was shining, yet he had often scorched past me on wet days.

'I hear,' he said genially,' that you did some dramatic training in college.'

'I did some training in Rural Science, too,' I told him, 'but everything.I planted died.'

He ignored this sally.

'We were thinking of putting on a bit of a play,' he said off-handedly. 'The Building Fund, you know. It'll take a power of money to carry out the programme.'

'And what,' I asked somewhat sarcastically, 'has all this to do with me?'

The mask of geniality vanished instantly.

'I'm the chairman of the Dramatic Society,' he snapped, 'but I'm far too busy, what with the new shop and one thing or another, to produce a play this year. You can produce it. There's nothing to it.'

I played my Johnston-type trump card.

'Why me?'

'You have the training,' he scowled at me, 'and what's more, you have the time. There'll be a meeting tonight. My house, eight o'clock.'

Gerry had not provided me with a suitably devastating reserve comeback and before I knew it I was standing on the kerb with one single thought in my mind. I was blowed if I was going anywhere near his house at eight o'clock.

And I didn't. I went at nine and I was far too early at that, for there was no one there but himself.

'Not many here,' I remarked maliciously and sat down unbidden.

'They'll be here soon,' he said sourly and added pointedly, 'some of them have been working.'

I was glad when he threw me a copy of the play, for I could see that the strain of the silence was likely to be too much for one of us, and there was no telling when the rest of the society would appear. I won't name the play, for in view of what we subsequently did with it, I have no wish to cause unnecessary suffering to its author, if he is alive, or to his heirs, successors or copyright holders if he is not. The play had a cast of seven and we had three scripts. I mentioned this obvious discrepancy and was immediately frowned upon.

'I got these in a job lot at an auction,' he said, yawning. 'Three's plenty.'

The author was not going to live heavily on the royalties from this production. A dramatic society which selected a play on the basis of having come into easy possession of three scripts for a cast of seven was likely to have free wheeling views on moneys due to the author. With some degree of malice I read out the conditions for stage production from the inside of the cover. The sometime producer looked at me in astonishment.

'Royalties!' he snorted. 'Balderdash!'

'That's immoral,' I informed him tartly, 'as well as illegal.' I felt I was on firm ground here. Building projects would require goods from his enterprises and the Canon was the paymaster. I was sure the Canon would take a dim view of this particular piece of rascality and I said so.

'Look,' he said patiently, 'it's only a bit of a play in a village hall and your man,' he waved his copy of the script in the air, 'lives somewhere in the Free State. He'll never know.'

I was outraged at this parsimonious attitude and expressed the pious wish that any edifice partly built from funds raised from this production would fall, preferably on top of certain persons I didn't wish to name just then.

'All right,' he snapped, 'if you feel that way about it, you pay the bloody thing then.'

'All right,' I snapped back, 'I will.'

At this juncture two more members of the society arrived. Indeed it turned out that the Dramatic Society consisted of just the four of us: Johnny McCloskey, a small, balding, bespectacled, easy-going local character called Larry Mooney, the literary bandit turned ex-producer and myself. Johnny was another junior teacher who threw himself with cynical enthusiasm into all local projects that took his fancy. He pulled his chair close to mine.

'Did you,' he asked with a conspiratorial grin, 'get stung for the royalties? Well, cheer up, it was my turn last year.'

Before I could fully grasp the neat way I had been manoeuvred into this particular corner, we were in the midst of a lively discussion on the casting of the play. The plot was simple enough. There were two brothers, that was Johnny and me, and a sister who had yet to be found, all living on one farm. The sister was a bossy piece who made life awkward for the two of us, and to make matters worse there was no great rush of suitors for her. Not, that is, until word got out that she had inherited some land. This brought the elderly but land-hungry bachelor, played by Larry, into the picture. There was a complication, of course, in that the land was a fiction invented by Johnny and me to get her off our hands so that we could marry a couple of lassies yet to be cast. I've never been exactly sure what is meant by a hollow laugh, but I fancy it's the sound I emit when I hear or read of people jockeying for power or parts in an amateur dramatic society. Horse-trading and Mafia-type intrigue do not take place within the ranks. I've never heard anyone complain bitterly or even mildly about someone else being given a leading part. In my experience, if scheming and plotting do take place, it's only in the producer's fevered brain as he strives to find enough people to fill the cast-list, for people have an understandable reluctance to make a spectacle of their blood and bones on the stage of the local hall, just to entertain their friends and neighbours. Large attendances at rural amateur dramatic presentations are made up of people who have come to see a shambles and to support the worthy cause, strictly in that order.

I acquired another seven scripts by telephoning a college friend in Belfast and begging him to chase them up round the bookshops. They duly arrived, accompanied by a bill with 'Serves you right' scrawled across it in red marker. Now the process of casting could begin, for I reasoned that without enough scripts to go round, nothing short of blackmail — and I hadn't been around long enough to get the goods on anyone — would induce people to accept a part.

I finally got seven people together, and cast the play by the simple process of typecasting. We needed a sharp-tongued lady for one part and recruited one such. We needed an extrovert type for another, so we persuaded such a girl to accept a part. It didn't work out. The virago, as soon as she set foot on the stage became totally refined and useless. The extrovert became tongue-tied even in the presence of Larry, who seldom turned up for rehearsal and never learned a line. He would march on stage in fine feather, stop dramatically, place the tips of the fingers of his right hand over his right eye, droop his left hand, dying-swan-style and become rigid. This was the signal that he had dried up, which of course he had not. To dry up you need to have learnt something and Larry didn't go in for mundane things like that. His reputation as a great actor, and the term was actually applied to him, was founded on a part he had played in *Arsenic and Old Lace,* while he had been living in another part of the country. Nobody had seen him in the play, and it would be charitable to assume he had played a corpse. Certainly it could have been nothing requiring either physical or mental effort, for Larry was one of nature's engaging rascals and all he ever played was himself.

Rehearsals staggered on for a couple of weeks during which I aged prematurely and considerably. The cast had to be treated with kid gloves, not because of artistic temperament, but simply because at least four of them were under duress and were looking for a suitable excuse to renege. There was no question of even mildly referring to people being an hour late for rehearsal, no gentle reproof for failure to learn lines. It took only one outburst of you-know-what-you-can-do-with-your-rotten-play from one of our mutinous cast and the whole production foundered. There was another complication, one for which we could blame the author, although that was unfair for he couldn't possibly have had our dramatic society in mind when he wrote his play. There was a line in the first act very similar to one in the third, and it fell to Larry to deliver it. Without fail, at every rehearsal he attended, Larry plunged straight on into the third act from this point. I could see a certain merit in this. By lopping off the second part of the first act, all of the second and the first half of the third, we could have shortened our own agony, as well as that of the audience, without diminishing their understanding of the plot, for with our level of expertise we could have made Jack and Jill incomprehensible. The audience, however, would expect two to three hours of entertainment, intentional or otherwise, and they would settle for nothing less.

If things were not complicated enough, the chairman appeared out of the blue — I hadn't seen him since the first meeting — and decreed that the play would have to be staged on the twenty-first. There was a sound, practical reason for this. His friend the auctioneer had exactly the right furniture in his store, but it was up for auction on the twenty-second. We had a seven-hander chosen because we had acquired three scripts, a date chosen because furniture was available then and only then, a cast verging on mutiny and a tacit understanding that we would provide our own costumes. This was no shoestring production, for there was neither shoe nor string.

It was duly staged on the twenty-first in the presence of every able-bodied man, woman and child in the village. By eight o'clock there wasn't even standing room in the hall, the show should have begun but Larry hadn't even arrived. The chairman arrived, greeted everybody perfunctorily and retreated into a corner of one of the two dressing rooms where he and the two volunteer stagehands were soon immersed in a game of poker, oblivious to all the bedlam around. At a quarter past eight Larry arrived. Just as he was leaving, he informed me, a visitor had arrived. You couldn't be ignorant, like, he explained, an' he thought she'd nivir go but dammit she did and sure nothin' ever starts on time an' nobody expects it. He didn't know a single line of the script. Even the title seemed to be giving him difficulty, and standing up was something of a problem too.

I stationed our three prompters right on the stage. One behind a sofa, one behind a dresser and one behind a fireplace. They were three sympathetic colleagues, recruited specifically to carry Larry safely through the minefield of the first act, all the way through the second and third, right to the final curtain. Forty-five minutes late, with a thought and a prayer, we launched the disaster. Never again will I believe that it will be all right on the night, for at the critical line, the bold Larry took off into the third act. All three prompters corrected in in thunderous stage whispers.

'Eh?' said Larry, mystified in the middle of the stage. Another thunderous prompt came from behind the sofa. Larry considered it with the air of a man who had never heard the line in his life, then frankly disbelieving he strode over to the sofa. A hand shot up bearing the script. Larry grabbed the wrist, with one hand, fumbled in his inside jacket pocket for his glasses with the other and then read the lines with mounting surprise. Then he turned to the audience, carefully removed his glasses and delivered the line in a you'll-never-believe-it-folks tone. A tidal wave of laughter washed over the stage.

Towards the end of the first act, Larry was supposed to exit to the yard, but he chose to exit to the bedroom. The door fell with a resounding crash and the audience hooted, but whether from derision or amusement, I never knew, for the wall followed immediately, entombing a prompter and revealing the ropes, pulleys and bric-a-brac that constitute the innards of a backstage. The curtain developed hiccups and was walked shut by the volunteer stage hands newly liberated from their poker game.

The ballot sellers moved swiftly among the audience selling cloak-room tickets at grossly inflated prices so that the audience would have the opportunity to win tins of biscuits extorted from village shop-keepers under heaven only knows what kind of blackmail. The audience turned the interval to good use by starting or completing deals to buy cattle, second-hand farm machinery or simply in criticising their neighbours, a pursuit in which the cast must have figured largely.

In the second act Larry was to stride on stage in a temper and read an important letter laying bare the machinations of the devious brothers. He strode on, produced a handful of nothing from his inner pocket and proceeded to read it. He couldn't remember what he was supposed to say but Johnny saved the day by marching on and thrusting a copy of the *Radio Times* into his hand with the explanation, 'You dropped this letter crossing the yard.' Larry duly read from the cover of the *Radio Times,* with the help of a prompter but without the aid of his glasses, an oversight the audience loudly drew to his attention.

In the third act, without any help from anywhere, our facsimile fireplace fell, revealing a prompter crouched apparently in prayer. In fact he was convulsed with laughter to the extent that he didn't even notice that his cover was blown. I achieved a brief moment of glory by putting my foot through a weak board on the stage and the leading lady tore a piece out of her dress on a projecting piece of the furniture destined for tomorrow's auction.

It dragged to its inglorious end and the Canon mounted the stage to pay tongue-in-cheek tribute to the herculean efforts of producer and cast. The audience remained stoically in position as the Canon, having disposed of the tributes and taking advantages of his captive audience, galloped away on one of his favourite hobby horses. I glanced along the line and could see only five of the cast. I addressed Johnny, who was shaking with laughter beside me.

'Where are the other two?' I whispered.

'Away home,' he answered, 'Good heavens, would anybody in their right mind want to be coming out of the hall at the same time as this crowd? You might never reach the corner.'

I could see his point. The banter would be savage if we had to run the gauntlet of the crowd outside as they stood finishing off deals, cigarettes and yarns. If we could escape now and only have to en-counter the playgoers in ones and twos through the countryside over the next week or two, the ordeal might not be too bad. I looked longingly into the wings.

'Away you go,' whispered Johnny, nudging me. I took a tentative step to one side, and from the tail of my eye I saw the right-hand flanker disappear. I hesitated no longer. Further delay and I could be the last one there. I left, followed immediately by Johnny. As we skulked down the path at the side of the hall, two shadowy figures emerged at the car-park entrance. For one panic-stricken moment I thought they were there to cut off our retreat, but they barely noticed us dodging past.

'I didn't know ye went in for this class of thing,' said one.

'I seldom do,' replied the other, 'but I hear Alec Murray has a trailer for sale and it wud save me a run out to his place if I could make a dale with him the night. Is he in there? I cudn't see him in the dark.'

'Oh, aye, he's there all right,' said the first. 'He'll be out as soon as His Reverence dries up.'

'Tell us,' said the second, 'what did ye think of the play?'

I froze in mid-step.

'Jizby,' said the second man, 'it's the best crack I seen in years. Thon Larry fella's a holy tara. Did ye see the cutta him stannin' there readin' thon book an' no specs on him? Sure the man cudn't find his face without his specs.'

I looked across at Johnny as the two men wandered on out of earshot.

'I think I've just learned a great truth,' I told him. 'We did what we were supposed to do, make cods of ourselves. Do you think maybe we left too soon?'

'Not damn likely,' said Johnny emphatically. 'Any later and Connolly's would be closed.'

We scuttled off to Connolly's and found the local sergeant in possession. He was standing in the middle of the floor, with the thumbs of his gloved hands hooked in his greatcoat pockets and the bar-top was suspiciously clear. He and Connolly had simply been passing the time of day in the empty bar.

'You were in the play?' he accused.

We admitted this.

'You'll want a drink after that,' said the sergeant and adjusted his cap with meticulous care. 'You might even want two.' He went out.

'He missed his vocation,' I said to Johnny. 'He should have been a drama critic.'

'He's not a damned heretic,' said Connolly, whose hearing and appreciation of drama were both apparently deficient. 'He's a dacent man an' nivir misses church on a Sunday.'

'We'll drink to that,' I said peaceably.

Crafty Moves

It was a Monday morning near the end of a month that had lasted much longer than the salary cheque. The rain was lashing the asphalt playground and dripping sneeringly from the trees opposite the staff-room window. The smell of wet coats filled the corridor and the elderly Ford had refused point-blank to start. It was, I thought gloomily, the start of a week that could only get better since it could hardly get worse. But herein I was wrong. Bone-dry and indecently cheerful the principal emerged from his new Morris and invaded the staffroom.

'Good-morning,' he said and drew no reply from me for I was far too junior to correct him. I concentrated instead on a huddle of dejected children clustered round the door, waiting hopefully for the bell to ring and end their sodden misery. The principal tried again.

'I hope you have remembered this weekend's craft exhibition,' he said and I knew immediately the cause of his happiness. I was about to be caught out in yet another sin of omission. I had forgotten about the exhibition. I had been told about it, of course, in a roundabout kind of way for he never issued instructions directly in the matter of what I should or should not teach, but I had treated his previous remarks as statements of general interest. The creative deity had jestingly endowed me with two left hands with five thumbs on each and the fact was well-known, especially in the college I had recently left.

'There's only this week left,' he went on happily. 'Exhibits must be on display by five o'clock on Friday in Gerry Johnston's school.'

'There'll be no exhibits from my class,' I said rebelliously.

He was shocked.

'The parents will expect to see the work of their children on display,' he stated firmly. 'There is a tradition of it. Their friends and neighbours will all be there to see the exhibits and it could cause embarrassment if there are no entries from your class.'

'There'll be a great deal more embarrassment if there are,' I protested weakly. 'I know nothing about crafts.'

'I'm quite sure,' he said with authority, 'that you will come up with something.'

Something in his voice told me that pleading total indifference would not get me off the hook, so I duly grovelled and went off to my class and informed them that they were expected to make an exhibition of themselves the following Saturday. They were delighted.

'Please Sir,' yelled somebody, 'Tommy got a second prize last year.'

'What for, Tommy?' I enquired without enthusiasm.

'A blackthorn stick, Sir,' said Tommy casually.

'How?' I asked, with a little more interest. It seemed to me that since blackthorn sticks grew in the hedges, the prize ought in justice to have gone to Mother Nature, although she might have been understandably peeved to find that her handiwork rated a mere second prize. Before the week was out I was to learn that justice had little to do with exhibitions of rural craftwork.

'I just cut it and seasoned it up the chimney and varnished it,' said Tommy nonchalantly and I was relieved to find that my predecessor had not been too closely involved. Anna struck a blow for female equality.

'Doreen got a second prize, too,' she announced, scowling in Tommy's direction.

'Well, Doreen,' I asked benignly, 'what did you get your prize for?'

'Crochet.' Doreen never used two words if one or less would do. The room spun gently from side to side. I could conceivably assist in affronting Mother Nature and her works, but crochet, for heaven's sake, I could barely spell the word. I looked carefully at the class and they looked innocently back. For the first time I realised fully why schools began their day with a prayer. I composed my thoughts and prayed for miracles.

'Who,' I asked with studied carelessness, 'taught you crochet?'

'Me mammy,' was the brief but delightfully reassuring reply. I began to see that the fruits of home industry could be passed off in a face-saving operation. My own contribution to the exercise could be limited to labelling and transporting. It was then that an evil chance placed a ludicrous ambition in my head, for when I opened the drawer to get the register, I found the book.

When I had first taken up my appointment in the school I had brought along an impressive array of books as proof of my erudition and one of them was a slim manual of do-it-yourself bookbinding. It was not mine, I hasten to add, but belonged to a college room-mate and had become inexplicably included with my own books when I left. I had laid it aside with the intention of sending it to him, but as all who borrow or lend books know only too well the gap between intention and accomplishment is seldom bridged. Now as I saw it, a lunatic plan leaped into my mind. I would enter a bookbinding exhibit. In the forest of rag dolls and table mats that would constitute the hard core of the exhibition, this exhibit would stand out like a beacon. The judges would be irresistibly drawn to it. They would exclaim in rapture at its perfection, shower awards upon it and thank their lucky stars for having had the honour to judge such a rare exhibit.

There were one or two minor snags, of course, not the least of which was my total ignorance of bookbinding, but I did not intend to allow such a minor detail to cloud my dream. Even in my inexperience I knew that ignorance of a subject seldom prevented teachers from teaching it, or at least pontificating on it. I resolved forthwith to read The Book.

I decided to confer on Doreen, the crochet prizewinner, the honour of binding the book. She was unimpressed by the news, to the extent that she didn't even bother to ask me what bookbinding meant. She was a taciturn child and I notched the first score up to her, for my idea in choosing her was to try and draw her into some prolonged conversation. All the others in the class expressed their views at considerable and vigorous length on all manner of subjects, but Doreen confined herself to cryptic utterances of the most essential type. She displayed not the least curiosity about the undertaking, and my enthusiastic predictions of the excitement her masterpiece would elicit produced no more than a sidelong look clearly conveying her intention to humour my eccentricity, nothing more.

There were other minor difficulties. The school possessed no guillotine, strawboard or press. The manual was prepared to compromise, however. A sharp knife and a steel ruler would do the work of a guillotine, and two drawing boards with the book sandwiched between them and placed under Andy's considerable posterior would give that youth his first constructive role in the school's affairs.

He would save me the inconvenience, not to say expense, of having to find a press. Strawboard was found by the simple convenience of vandalising a ring binder. With blatant disregard for the instructions, a proprietary glue from the hardware shop was substituted for the recommended adhesive, a length of white lint bandage did duty for holding the edges of the pages together at the spine and the infants' teacher provided a suitable, gaily-coloured paper for the binding.

The project was a success. The taciturn Doreen was a neat, methodical and painstaking worker, as befitted a veteran of the crochet wars, and in two days time we had a twenty-four page book that would have been a credit to someone twice her tender years. The class was impressed. I was impressed. The principal was impressed. Then Tommy, of blackthorn stick fame, introduced a discordant note.

'There's nothing written in it,' he pointed out, with devastating practicality. I had, in my enthusiasm, entirely overlooked this important detail. A blank book would hardly set the judges' imaginations aflame.

Then the evil imp that first put the notion in my head popped up again to remind me that I owned an italic pen. In a brief moment of temporary fervour I had bought one while a student but as it is an instrument that slows one down, I had reverted to my customary ballpoint scrawl after a week or two. A frantic search of my cases and boxes unearthed the pen and a bottle of Indian ink, so with two days to go I presented it to Doreen and gave her a demonstration of its uses. Half an hour later, without a word of comment, she placed upon my desk a copy of 'The Lake Isle of Innisfree', written in beautiful italic script and I cheered inwardly. There was to be no stopping the talented Doreen. By three o'clock on Friday, each right-hand page had a verse in italic script, the first few pages being occupied by the Lake Isle. By five o'clock on Friday, the newly-bound book was prominently displayed in one of the two classrooms allocated by Gerry Johnston for the exhibition.

I had brought along the usual assortment of table mats, rickety teapot stands, harvest bows and other standard bric-a-brac of the rural craft scene. Tommy, who possessed neither the silence nor adaptability of his sister, insisted on entering his blackthorn stick again.

I remonstrated about the propriety of this move but he dismissed my objections with 'Ah, sure they'll never remember it from last year.'

To tell the truth, I feared nature's memory more than the judges' but I let it pass. The bookbinding exhibit, in my totally biassed view, overshadowed all other items.

The judging was to take place the next day at noon, and I had every intention of being there. But the road to craft exhibitions is paved with good intentions and that Friday was payday. An evening of celebration followed by a dance in the Castle in Dungiven which ended at two in the morning was part of the problem. An ancient Standard Ten that refused point-blank to carry eight of us, or even one of us along with the driver, up the mile-long climb of Tamneyarn also played a significant role in my missing the judging. The car eventually arrived at the top, having been reversed the whole way and collected a flat wheel halfway up. It was broad daylight when I got to bed and after lunch-time when I surfaced. I reached the centre just after two to find Tommy and his cohorts decorating the ancient water-pump facing the door. Tommy's dog, a genetic patchwork of a creature, was blocking the entrance.

'We didn't get many prizes,' one of them announced mutinously and the rest of them muttered ominously. The dog growled in sympathy and walloped the door with a club-like tail.

'Please sir,' another said consolingly, 'Tommy got a second for his blackthorn.'

I flinched somewhat and glanced uneasily upwards, but Mother Nature was busy elsewhere. No thunderbolt descended. Not yet anyway.

'Aye, that's all right,' said Tommy, 'but I didn't see our Doreen's book anywhere.'

They looked at me expectantly and the dog gave an accusing growl. I charged into the centre and made straight for the spot I had placed the book. It was nowhere to be seen. In its place stood the most hideous cushion I have ever seen in my life, and a quick tour of the room revealed not a trace of my pride and joy. Mother Nature, I felt at that moment, had her revenge.

My pupils stood in a tight knot at the door of the otherwise empty room as I made a second tour of the exhibits. This time I found the the book. It was lying closed under the cushion, which was not only by a school I had never even heard of, but also collected a first prize, proof positive of total blindness on the part of the judges. The exhibitor of the cushion had simply swept Doreen's masterpiece aside and placed her hideous creation on top of it. I marched into the other room in a towering rage and found Gerry Johnston drinking a cup of tea and reading the paper.

'You appear to be very unhappy with life today,' he remarked. 'What has happened? Or not happened, as the case may be?'

'Come into the other room a minute,' I invited and he followed me to where the cushion reposed. We both looked at it for a moment in awe-struck silence.

'What is it?' he asked at length. 'Is it dead, do you think?'

'It's a cushion,' I informed him. He poked it experimentally.

'Are you sure?' he asked. 'You could catch something dreadful if you sat on a thing like that.'

'It look as if it was made by a blacksmith using a knife and fork,' I said.

'If you threw it into Loch Ness,' said Gerry thoughtfully, 'it would scare the monster out.' He read the label.

'Ah,' he said, 'the Maghera Marauder strikes again. I should explain to you that there are about thirty prizes in this exhibition. The lady who teaches the child who produced that... cushion... annually collects about a third of them. The other umpteen schools get the rest.'

'How does she do it?' I wanted to know.

'Well, one of the judges has bad eyesight, and one is believed to be related. She probably has some terrible hold over the third. She is built,' he went on, 'along the lines of the *Ark Royal,* and she stands by the door when the judging is going on, breathing heavily all the time. Observers claim to see smoke issuing from her nostrils occasionally. No judge would willingly cross her.'

I picked up the cushion and revealed the bookbinding exhibit.

'Look,' I said, 'I don't care who gets what or where, but there's a fine piece of bookbinding and italic script, and it's been literally overthrown to make way for this horrible object.'

'I see,' said Gerry thoughtfully. 'You're not entirely disinterested, then. Still, I see the reason for your disappointment. There has been a miscarriage of justice, without a doubt. Let me see,' and he wandered off round the two rooms.

'The Marauder has collected eleven prizes,' he said thoughtfully. 'I have to write to them all informing them of their good fortune.'

'Does she,' I asked carefully, 'know exactly who has won what?'

'No,' said Gerry, with equal care. 'She stayed at the door.'

'There is another copy of this list?'

'No.'

I looked at Gerry.

'?'

He looked blandly back at me.

'!'

'It would be a service to generations yet unborn,' I intoned solemnly as he rubbed industriously and substituted Doreen's name, in carefully forged handwriting. 'If the *Ark Royal* got away with that she would flood the country with rubbish like it.'

He looked at me with one eye shut, a curious mannerism he had.

'She's been flooding the place with rubbish for years,' he said drily.

I switched the prize stickers round and went back to my pupils at the door.

'It was a slight mistake,' I lied cheerfully. 'Mr Johnston says the labels were put on the wrong objects. Doreen has won first prize. Mr Johnston,' I added brazenly, 'has the correct list.'

Their whoops of delight could be heard all over the village as they trooped in to view the exhibition again. Gerry and I were taking a leisurely look around the other room when a frantic racket broke in the room we had just left. We raced back in time to see Tommy's dog drag the cushion to the floor and for reasons that will be forever locked in his canine brain, proceed to kill it. It took the combined efforts of Tommy, Gerry and myself to wrest the now ragged exhibit from him.

'Take him home,' said Gerry, who was, among other things, very fond of dogs. 'He's an excellent judge of rural craftwork and I wouldn't want him to get sick, or heaven forbid, die, not in my school.'

I cannot honestly say that our devious ploy had totally escaped detection. We had left no evidence but something happened the following month which made me think.

All the teachers in the locality were invited to a lecture in the local technical school and I found myself sitting beside Gerry immediately behind a row of young and giggling lady teachers. A few moments before the speaker mounted the platform a formidable lady came and sat in front of us. Suddenly she turned and addressed Gerry with chilling cheerfulness.

'Well, Mr Johnston,' she boomed. 'What are you doing these days for diversion?'

Gerry eyed her disarmingly.

'I've just been initiating our young colleague here into my hobby of inventing collective nouns,' he said, indicating the lady teachers in front. 'For example, a giggle of lady teachers.'

She leaned back, just as the speaker rose, and gave him a meaningful look.

'I have another for your collection,' she hissed. 'For principals. A lack of.'

I slid down out of sight.

'I think,' said Gerry to me, Bogart-style, 'that she had the last word.'

'You may be right,' I conceded happily. 'But who got the prize?'

The Wake

It was morning break and we were sitting round the staffroom table drinking that curious brew that passes for tea in most educational establishments. The principal looked at me over his glasses.

'Are you doing anything special tonight?' he asked.

'No,' I replied innocently. I was getting tired of my diet of baked beans and similar bachelor convenience foods, and the principal's wife was a splendid cook. But there was to be no free handout at the principal's bungalow and I was soon to learn the hard way that jumping to conclusions is a futile exercise for mind or body.

'Good,' said the principal, cheerfully. 'The wife and I are going away this weekend and there's Paddy McKelvey's wake to go to.'

'That's awkward,' I said sympathetically. The demise of Paddy McKelvey, inconvenient though it might be for many, including Paddy, had little to do with me that I could see. I had never met the man, not to my knowledge.

'Well,' said the principal carefully, 'one of us ought to go to the wake. It's the custom. He has relations at the school, you see.'

I didn't see, but I said I did. The boss is the boss is the boss and if he had booked a weekend break it seemed prudent not to get in the way of his pleasure.

'I'll go, if you like,' I volunteered. The principal feigned grateful surprise.

'That's grand,' he said. 'If you're sure...'

'Oh, yes, it's no trouble,' I lied cheerfully and stumped off to my classroom. Not for the first time it crossed my mind that a country schoolmaster had not only to be a jack of all trades, but he should also be available twenty-five hours a day, eight days a week.

On my way to the wake that night I stuck my head into Connolly's and found Johnny McCloskey, another slightly less junior teacher, perched on a high stool lecturing a bemused farmer on the merits of raising rabbits commercially.

'Rabbits is varmints,' said the farmer decisively. 'Any man that meets a rabbit, shud it be in Africa, shud kill it at wanst. Sure they do damn all but bore holes in the groun' for cattle to break their legs in. No amount of rabbits is worth a good cow an' that's that.'

'Well, what about mink then?' Johnny asked, grinning.

'What the hell's mink?' demanded the farmer.

Johnny turned and spotted me. 'Ha,' he said happily, 'here's a mourner on his way to the wake.'

'How did you know?' I asked sourly.

'You have that stag-at-bay look found only on the faces of junior teachers whose bosses have gone away for the weekend,' he informed me learnedly. 'And before they went they conned their weary assistants into deputising for them.'

'You too?' I asked hopefully.

'Me too,' said Johnny, indicating to the barman that strong drink was required.

'If,' I asked tentatively, 'it was a wedding, or a party, do you think...'

'Not on your life,' said Johnny with conviction. 'My man's at a wedding feast. Up in Tirboy,' he added meaningly.

'What's so special about Tirboy weddings?' I asked.

'It's poteen country. They make a brew up there that the experts can't tell from gin. He'll be there tomorrow too. He'll be a wheelbarrow case by Sunday morning. We'll have a couple of noggins before we head up the brae.'

'So we get the wakes and they get the weddings, is that it?' I asked, for the sake of clarification.

'Don't knock the wakes,' said Johnny, who could find amusement in any situation. 'You can have grand crack at some of them. I was at one last February when two of the family fell out over the will. They knocked hell out of each other up and down the yard. Then the family dogs fell out and fought each other and when they got tired of that they bit the two boyos rolling on the ground. A great night that was.'

'There's not a word of a lie in it, Master,' said the farmer to me. 'I was there meself. We got buckets of water to throw them over the dogs an' av coorse the pair of boys on the groun' got wet an' they got up to bate everybody. It was the best crack I've seen since Duffy's circus.'

'Well,' I said, not believing either of them, 'let's have another and get on up to the wake.'

The farmer wasn't going, having discharged his neighbourly obligations by 'sitting up' the previous night, so we set off up the hilly road in the moonlight.

'I don't know any of these people,' I said to Johnny. 'What's the drill, anyway?'

'Simple,' said Johnny. 'I'll go first. You shake hands with everybody I shake hands with, tell them you're sorry for their trouble, slither into a seat and take care you don't end up sitting next to some doting parent or you'll spend the night being grilled about his child's progress at school. Or lack of it, as the case may be.'

We came into the house on the heels of the local blacksmith, a small square character with impressively big feet. He had his cap under his arm and he greeted each relation at the door with a mournful expression and muttered platitude. He then disappeared into a crowded room where his appearance was greeted with delight, for he had an impressive line in wisecracks. We entered somewhat more decorously.

'Two schoolmasters, begod,' muttered a voice in the crowd and I could see that regardless of what our principals may have thought of us, our arrival lent some class to the proceedings. Johnny ploughed on into the room and I slid into the nearest vacant seat.

'Scotch?' hissed a voice in my ear, and a full tumbler of same was thrust at me. Before I could say anything, the donor had plunged into the crowd with a bottle in one hand and five glasses in the other. In no time at all he was back, this time with a plate on which there were about forty cigarettes of the variety known locally and appropriately as coughin' nails.

'The hospitality is lavish,' I said to my neighbour. He indicated a Pioneer pin in his lapel.

'He offered me a tumblerful, too, when I came in,' he laughed. 'When I said I was a total abstainer, he wanted me to take a bottle of stout instead.'

'Right, Master,' said the bottle-bearer, appearing before me like the genie of the lamp. 'Come on for a bite to ate.'

He took a firm grasp of my arm and propelled me from my seat across the hall into the parlour. It was a big room, with a long table running along each side. Each table was surrounded by chairs and covered with white tablecloth. Mourners were evidently not going to perish from malnutrition for the centre of each table was lined with plates of sandwiches, pastry and cakes, while two decidedly able-bodied ladies stood before the fire with huge teapots at the ready. Two men in suits but wearing clay-clogged wellingtons sat sideways at one table, demolishing platefuls of bacon and eggs.

'Much trouble sinkin' the grave?' enquried my Pioneer neighbour.

'Damn the bit,' one of them belched affably and I noticed that his affability stemmed from the fact that he had forsworn the large teacup and was washing down his fry with a tumblerful of seventy proof. I wondered idly what convention dictated that suits should be worn while digging a grave, but laid the thought aside and concentrated on a remarkable tribute being paid to the quality of the sandwiches by a little man opposite me. He carefully removed his dentures and placed them on his plate, but thought better of that and wrapped them instead in a grimy handkerchief. This precaution completed, he proceeded to demolish his sandwiches with truly impressive speed. For some curious reason my appetite vanished.

'Ye're not atin' much, Master,' one of the teapot-wielding ladies reproved. 'Sure them wee picks of things is no good to a fella your size.'

She picked up a selection of the sandwiches and placed them on my plate with a no-nonsense flourish and bulldozed amiably round the table ordering everyone to eat up.

'If you hear a rattle or two upstairs,' said my teetotal neighbour, 'it'll be Paddy spinnin' in his coffin.'

'Why should he do that?' I asked.

'You didn't know him,' said the teetotaller. 'There's more spent in this house the night than he spent in his whole life.'

'He wasn't a big spender then?' I asked.

'Spend!' he laughed. 'The first bob he ever made is wrapped in tissue paper in his waistcoat pocket, if you could only see it. Thank God none of his relatives took after him.'

'You know the family well, then?' I said, just to keep the conversation moving. He gave me a sidelong look.

'I married the daughter,' he said cryptically. Never say anything to anybody about anybody, you never know who you're talking to, the principal had once advised me. I could see the value of the advice at that moment.

We left the table to make room for the next relay and as I passed the kitchen I could see Johnny energetically hindering a number of giggling girls at their conveyor-belt sandwich-making operation. In the other room I sat down beside a stout man in a brown suit. Too late I realised, that with the whole room to pick from, I had chosen to sit beside the father of Andy, who had lectured me on educational reform on my first day. He leaned over ominously, and I could detect that he had been mourning for some time.

'Ye know what it is, Master,' he said to me confidentially. 'Schoolin' can be a costly business.'

He eyed me as one who has the inside information, so it seemed to me to be diplomatic to agree. It would, I felt sure, be a far-ranging discussion in which I was not equipped to have the last word.

I had been through it once or twice before and the topic could be the wastage of public money on educating a lot of idlers, or the unnecessarily high rates of salaries paid to teachers who after all only worked half the day/week/year, if in fact they could be said to work at all. There was also the ridiculous cost of rates or schoolbags to be considered. So I supposed he was right in his assertion. Past experience had taught me that I was likely to be held responsible for the high cost of whatever it was. He was an ex-corporal of Signals, World War One variety, and in a community where no one else had ever attained that exalted rank, he was a person of consequence and a grateful nation had rewarded him with a labouring job with the council. He had also acquired a remarkably ill-fitting set of false teeth — on no account did they merit the description of dentures — sometime in his career, so the conversation with him was punctuated with sounds, which, had they emanated from behind a hedge on a dark night, would have been worrying in the extreme. Ever since that night I have somewhat morbidly associated false teeth and wakes.

'Aye,' he went on, 'it can be a dear business sending a lad to school these days.' He tilted his head on one side, burrowed fervently in a hairy nostril, sniffed and regarded me challengingly.

'But,' I protested, 'nobody pays directly for schooling these days.'

'I do,' he stated flatly. 'That Andy fella is costin' me a fortune.'

'But Andy is in my class,' I protested again. 'What expense is there in that?'

'Bathroom windas,' stated the ex-corporal enigmatically. 'An' glass is dear.'

I had difficulty in associating the cost of glass with the cost of education and even more in associating the said Andy with a bathroom.

46

Not that he didn't have access to a bathroom, for he lived in the council estate, but whatever obscure rituals Andy may have carried out in that modern convenience, washing was not one of them. It was the principal's considered opionion that if all the external layers of grime could have been stripped off Andy, with the help of a sander, he usually added, he would have shrunk noticeably.

He did need to shrink, too, because he was the second biggest boy in the school and still only in Primary Six. This was quite something, for our school was of the unreorganised variety and we catered for all up to leaving age. It was the principal's fixed rule that nobody moved up a class until they had reached the standard required for that class, and since there was no possibility of Andy ever reaching anything except possibly the lintel of the school door, it looked as if he would attain leaving age without ever leaving Primary Six.

'Y'see,' the father continued. 'He doesn't like school.'

A perfectly reasonable dislike, all thing considered. After all, if you're five foot and a bit and trapped in Primary Six, the establishment is bound to have little appeal. I kept this piece of philosophy to myself.

'I can't get him outta bed in the mornin',' the father continued. 'I jist take a good hoult o' the mattress and pitch him out on the floor. An' then bedammit he makes for the bathroom and boults the dure. Four times the past twelvemonth I had to break the bathroom winda to get in at him. It's a dear business I can tell ye. Tell us, has he any brains at all?'

If Andy's brains had been damp gelignite they would have posed no threat whatever to his cap, but it's not the done thing to send people away with a sad heart, so I waffled on at length about the need for hewers of wood and drawers of water and their vital place in society. The father nodded sagely from time to time and continued to explore his nose. He alternated this activity with determined prospecting in an equally hairy ear, holding up the fruits of his efforts for inspection before disposing of them on the leg of his trousers. I found concentration difficult in the circumstances. Indeed I wondered if I was merely providing a background noise as he carried out his cleansing operations. Eventually he decided that he had heard enough of my theorising and he held up an imperious hand.

'Tell us, Master,' he commanded. 'Has he any chance of this qualifyin' exam at all?'

It was a question to which there was literally no answer. It was fortunate that at that moment a stray puff of smoke went down my throat and turned my potentially hysterical guffaw into a strangled sob. On the pretext of needing air I stumbled, coughing exaggeratedly, out into the yard. As I went, the da addressed the gathering in general.

'What the hell's he talkin' about? Sure our houses all have the watther in them,' he announced, triumphantly.

Outside I found Johnny and one of the giggling girls from the kitchen conveyor belt concluding negotiations, at close quarters, about a dance the following night.

'You going home?' Johnny asked over her shoulder. 'Well, walk slowly, I'll catch up with you.'

I dandered slowly down the hill road, looking down at the lights of the village and soon heard footsteps hurrying behind me. It was the diminutive blacksmith.

'Did ye enjoy the crack?' he asked, falling into step.

I mentioned that I hadn't known the deceased personally. The blacksmith sniffed a couple of times and spat.

'Ye didn't miss much, an' I shudn't spake ill o' the dead. He was a tight man wi' the bob. The rest o' them's all right, dacent people but he was as mane as get-out. Y'know, the first time he built on a bit to the house an' that's not the day nor yesterday, he got me brother the carpenter to make the windas. When the brother asked him for measurements, he jist says make them good an' big for light's chape. An' begod it was chape, too, for he's waitin' yit for the money.'

I could only laugh, for the story was told without malice, almost with admiration. Johnny came trotting up behind us.

'What's the laugh?' he demanded.

'I was jist sayin' to the Master here,' said the blacksmith, 'that if I had big long legs like you, I could run after the weemin too.

Johnny was one of those rare people who could say anything to anyone and get away with it, and he clapped the blacksmith cheerfully on the shoulder.

'Do you know what, John,' he said seriously, 'if they hadn't turned so much of you up for feet, you could catch them, too.'

Called to the Harvest

'D'ye know what it is,' said Connolly to me at the school gate, 'the world is ill-divid. There's people,' he went on unctuously, 'that work, work, I'm tellin' ye, with their coats aff, from mornin' till night. An' then there's others, mentionin' no names, that gets two months, two whole bloody months holidays, paid in full begod, and them with damn the hate to do but watch the rest of us workin'. The world's ill-divid.'

He mourned the injustice of it all with a mischievous grin on his face. The school had just closed for the summer holidays and I had been making my inopportune exit just as Connolly drove past in his van.

'Jealousy'll get you nowhere,' I informed him grandly. 'If you want to be one of the idle poor, sell all thou hast and give it to me.'

'No coddin',' said Connolly, getting out of the van. 'Many a wan like ye wud give a fella a han'.'

'What sort of a hand?' I demanded suspiciously. 'If you mean work, let me tell you I think it's vastly overrated as a way of passing the time. I've seen a lot of it in my time and no good ever came of it.'

'Lissen,' said Connolly, 'lissen here a minute. I'm serious. There's you, young an' strong an' fit with nothin' to do for two months, an' there's me with the hay an' the turf to get an' no help.'

'The heart bleeds at your predicament,' I told him. 'Are you making me some sort of proposition, by any chance?'

He walked away a few steps and walked back jingling his loose change.

'Well,' he said, 'I'm sort of stuck, right enough. What with the shop an' the bar an' wan thing or another, I need a bit of help to get the farm work done.'

'Tell me,' I asked in genuine curiosity, 'why do you still cut turf and you a local coal supplier? What sort of quack doesn't believe in his own medicine?'

'Ah, sure I only cut the turf for the crack, an' if I get them, sure there's no fire like a turf fire,' he told me without a trace of shame.

He walked his ritual couple of steps back and forth, jingling his money and looking sideways at me. For my part I was not inclined to take his proposition too seriously, for most nights of the week his bar was thronged with people better qualified in haymaking and turf-harvesting than I could ever be. He was also known for a somewhat puckish sense of humour, and the thought crossed my mind that maybe I was to be the victim of a rural practical joke of embarrassing dimensions.

'Well,' he said at last, 'will ye give me a couple of days or not?'

'Are you joking?' I asked.

'Lissen,' he said, 'if ye're scared of a bit of hard work...' He didn't finish.

'It's not that,' I half-lied, 'what about Frank?'

Frank was a dour, uncompromising man that a life of unremitting toil had converted into a smallish, slow-moving mass of muscle. He had worked for Connolly, to use one of his own expressions, since pussy was a cat; indeed he regarded all Connolly's hard labour as his own prerogative, and the arrangement suited Connolly, for Frank drank most of his remuneration at his employer's counter. At a certain stage in the drinking, he would inform the world at large that he had personally been the making of Connolly. Not only had he run his farm for him, but he had also drunk four thousand, or ten thousand, or some other equally large and round figure, gallons of his beer, which was more than anyone else was capable of doing. He always looked belligerently round as he quoted his figures but no one ever challenged him, for he was among other things, a lifelong and methodical hater. Once on the wrong side of Frank you stayed there.

'Frank won't like it,' I said.

'He'll be glad of the help,' said Connolly dismissively. 'He's not the man he used to be, but nobody about here cud work with him. He doesn't know you, so ye might manage it.'

'Connolly,' I said, not entirely happy at being a pawn in the labour relations game, 'you drive a hard bargain for cashing a man's cheques.'

'Lissen,' said Connolly, 'if I cashed any more cheques for you fellas, I'd have to score out Bar and put Bank over the window. Boys I'd be in the quare oul' pucker if the bank started to sell drink or groceries.'

'Or coal,' I pointed out but he let the sarcasm pass.

I was wrong when I said that Frank wouldn't like the arrangement. He was in fact openly contemptuous when I presented myself at the hayfield the next morning and he returned my civil greeting with a sizzling, splendiferous gobbet of tobacco juice that annihilated a colony of grasshoppers and stained a square foot of lush green grass a dirty brown. He handed me a pitchfork and set a cracking pace along a windrow of hay, his fork blurred like a propeller as the hay shot into the air and fell green side up. It was a blistering hot day, and it was more than a little uncomfortable, with the sweat, the hostile silence and my own lack of practice at the work. The year's teaching had not, fortunately, entirely cancelled out the entire muscular improvements of three summers spent navvying and it was with well-concealed exultation that I saw Frank stick the pitchfork in the ground and announce that it was time for a smoke.

As we sprawled in the shade of the ash-trees that lined the field the only sound came from a lone grasshopper that had survived Frank's saturation blitzkrieg, and I did not find it reassuring. Like the man in the story, I dearly loved a conversation, intelligent if possible but failing that, any sort would do. The prospect of several days of silence was distinctly unappealing. As I looked up into the distant blue, my morose reverie was shattered by a piercing scream. I shot upright.

'Razus,' screeched Frank, pop-eyed with horror. Razus was a popular local cussword of obscure origin.

'Razus!' he screeched again, holding up a brown and wiry arm. 'A bloody tick, bogged to the ass in me arm!'

I realised at that moment, if I ever doubted it before, that somewhere up in the bright blue yonder, there was a God and he loved me, for had he not shown me Frank's Achilles heel? The maker of Connolly's fortune was reduced to jelly by the common or garden tick. Something told me, as I plucked the offending bloated parasite from his arm, that Frank and I were the only two men alive who knew this potentially damaging fact.

He, for one, was never going to mention it. He extended his cigarette packet in token of peace and I looked him carefully in the eye as

51

I took one. Silence reigned again, this time of the companionable variety. We were two weary workers snatching a break while the boss had his back turned. I was in no way prepared for a second cry of 'Razus!'

'What is it this time?' I asked without opening an eye. 'Another tick?'

'Worse,' groaned Frank. 'God almighty, wud ye luk at this!'

I looked. Striding across the field towards us was a small man wearing a heel-length tweed overcoat on a day when a tee shirt would have been heavy.

'Name-a-God,' moaned Frank tragically, 'we'll nivir get ridda him.'

Ten yards from us the newcomer thrust his hands heavenwards and came to a halt.

'Repent!' he ordered grimly.

He was as broad as he was long and his brick-red face, sticking up from the heavy coat, was shaded by a greasy cap. He wore a collar and tie, both grimy, and his black shoes were, incongruously, gleaming. He looked from Frank to me and back again.

'Idlers,' he roared. This was, on the surface of it, true.

'Sinners!' he yelled. This, I felt, was open to debate. He swayed and clutched the lapels of the tweed overcoat in an effort to keep upright. When he moved his arms I spotted the neck of a John Powers bottle projecting from his pocket. Our missionary was as full as the tick I had excised from Frank's arm.

'I have travelled this day,' he intoned, holding himself up with one hand and gesturing with the other, 'from Portglenone, and everywhere I see idleness and sinfulness. Why are you men not earnestly working at the harvest as I am?'

'Are you any relation of Connolly's?' I asked.

He silenced me with a ferocious glare and tugged the Powers bottle from his pocket.

'Repent,' he commanded. 'There cometh one after me.'

'Definitely one of Connolly's spies,' I told Frank.

The missionary hunkered down facing us and drank deeply from his bottle.

'There will be a day of reckoning,' he informed us.

'Aye, the morra at quettin' time,' said Frank, sniggering.

'Repent!' snarled the missionary. 'There will be weeping and gn..na ..scringin' of teeth, so take heed.'

'Tell me,' I asked pleasantly, 'what would you like us to repent of? Just to begin with.'

He raised his eyebrows at me.

'Of sloth!' he snapped. 'The harvest is great and the labourers are few.'

'Ah, now houl' on,' said Frank testily. 'It's only a wee field an' there's two of us. Anyway, he's not a labourer, he's a schoolmaster.'

The missionary got on to all fours and struggled into something resembling the vertical position, from which he viewed us with contempt.

'I can see,' he said with drunken dignity, 'that my message is falling on stony ground. I'll wipe the dust of this place from my feet.'

'Aye, do,' growled Frank. 'Clear aff. There's neither stones nor dust in this field,' he added in the hurt tones of a fond mother who has just been told her child has lice.

The missionary lurched towards the gate, pausing when halfway there to issue one more injunction to repent.

'Who is he?' I asked.

'Ach, he's from down the country,' said Frank, as though this geographical distinction explained everything. 'They say he has a wee farm down there somewhere an' every time he falls behind with the work, he takes out on wan of them boozin', prachin' trips. He's as mad as bedamned.'

He got to his feet, spat on his hands and seized the pitchfork. I followed suit reluctantly.

'I was just thinking,' I said to Frank, just to try the atmosphere, 'wouldn't it be a laugh if he was sane and we were the crazy ones?'

He stared at me with open mouth and attacked the hay vigorously.

'Razus!' he said feelingly to the pitchfork. 'Bloody schoolmasters, they're worse nor the prachers.'

It was, as he said, a wee field and there were two of us, so by teatime the hay was safely in forkcocks and we were in Connolly's kitchen demolishing a substantial meal. The next day, Connolly informed us, we could foot the turf.

The next day it rained so we spent the morning loafing. More precisely I loafed while Frank, never one to waste an opportunity, sprawled in the bar and notched up a few more gallons to his score. I whiled away the time by reading the inspiring messages Connolly's well-meaning female ancestors had embroidered and framed, and by helping my temporary employer to unload a miscellaneous collection of nothing in particular from the van. Just before noon, the sky cleared and Connolly appeared from the kitchen with a bag containing the makings of a turf-cutter's lunch. For some inexplicable reason, nobody ever brought a flask and sandwiches to the turf, preferring instead to lug a bag containing a kettle, bread, butter, knives, spoons, tea, sugar, and jam, not to forget a considerable portion of grime, and dine alfresco on the turf bank. It was cumbersome, inefficient and totally sacred, this curious custom.

'Wud ye go in there an' throw Frank out,' said Connolly, settling himself in the driving seat, so I duly went and invited Frank to join us. He looked at me sourly.

'——off!' he said. 'It'll rain as soon as we get there, an' he'll be away with the van an' we'll get a soakin for damn all.'

The horn tooted imperiously.

'—— you too!' he yelled in the direction of the sound then suddenly something, possibly the memory of the tick, changed his mind and he lurched for the door. On the way out he grabbed a rain-coat from the hall. I was already equipped with an ancient model, for nobody ever went to the turf without being prepared for the worst.

He rolled his coat into a tight bundle and sat on it in the back of the van.

'Drive on, ye crabbit oul' twister, ye,' he said courteously to our employer.

The mountain, when we reached it, was devoid of humanity. The other turf workers had either gone home, or stayed there in the first place, and only a few sheep looked at us with dead eyes before point-edly turning their backs. The fog-like drizzle trailed back and forth like an ancient lace curtain.

'We'll go home,' announced Frank.

'We'll stay a while,' said Connolly. 'Maybe the sun'll come out again.'

'Ye're an eedjit, Connolly, d'ye know that,' growled Frank. 'Ye got no turf last year, ye'll get none this year and ye'll get none next year either.'

'He only cuts them for the crack,' I offered maliciously.

'What crack?' demanded Frank. 'Sure he nivir sets fut on the turf bank. I cut the bloody turf. Me an' some eedjit futs them. Me an' some other eedjit wheels them out an' stacks them. An' he laves them lyin' there till the next year. He's cracked.' He settled himself more comfortably on his makeshift cushion on the van floor. Connolly got out of the van and sank up to the laces of his boots in the sodden bog.

'Get in outta that,' Frank ordered his employer, rapping the side of the van. Connolly took another step and his boot, only loosely tied, was sucked off. In a frantic attempt to keep his balance he thrust his stockinged foot ankle-deep into the slimy bog.

'Razus!' roared Frank in exasperation. 'Ye're worse nor a wane. If ye get sucked down into that bog, how the hell will we get home?'

'If I were you, Frank,' I suggested, 'I'd give him the sack.'

'If he didn't pay the wages sort re'lar,' said Frank, 'I wud sack him. Get in, will ye.'

Connolly got in and ruefully studied the damage to his socks and boots. At that moment, the drizzle lifted and the sun appeared, lancing down that fierce heat you can only get between summer showers.

'It's a good day now,' said Connolly.

'Houl yer whist,' snapped Frank. 'It was a good day two or three times the day an' no matter what ye say, thon turf of yours won't be dry this year.'

'Well,' said Connolly, in a conciliatory tone, 'it won't do any harm to go over an' have a look at them, maybe turn them over. Luk, there's not a cloud. Tell ye what I'll do, you men go over and turn a few of them over an' I'll go back and change me boots an' socks. I'll be back in an hour or less.'

'What did I tell ye?' grumbled Frank to me, 'Damn the work he does at the turf. As soon as the sun comes out he's away home to dodge the work.'

'But me feet's wet,' said Connolly defensively.

'Aw, aye, surely,' sniffed Frank, getting out and dragging his coat after him. Connolly started up the van.

'Light the fire,' he said, preparing to drive off. 'Get the tay made. I'll be back when it's ready.'

He reversed away and left us standing on the edge of the bog, clutching the bag of makings and our raincoats.

'That's a very decent-looking coat to be bringing on a jaunt like this,' I said to Frank and he emitted a strangled yelp.

'Razus!' he screeched. 'It's Connolly's Sunday-go-to-meetin' coat. An' luk at the cut of it!'

He held it up for my inspection. It was wrinkled like a relief map from Frank's long session of sitting on it and it was generously stained by unidentifiable substances from the floor of the van.

'It's a new coat,' I said hopefully. 'If we spread it out carefully, the wrinkles might come out of it.'

He spread the coat out reverently on a patch of heather, and did up the buttons and the belt.

'Will it take the wrinkles long to come out?' Frank enquired.

'I don't know,' I answered truthfully. 'There's a worse problem. How will we hide it from Connolly when he comes back? Where do you hide a coat on a turf-bank?'

'Wan thing at a time,' announced Frank decisively. 'We'll get the

wrinkles out first. I might as well make the tay when we're waitin'.'
He proceeded to rifle a completed turf-stack for dry fuel and I made
myself useful by sawing up the bread and buttering it, all with the
help of a blunt bread-knife.

'Come on with me,' said Frank, picking up the kettle. 'I'll show ye
the purest watther in Ireland.'

We wandered off across the turf banks, two men in no hurry. In less
than ten minutes we arrived at a tiny spring no bigger than a basin.
The water was so clear the tiny pool seemed empty and still, apart
from the minute trickle that issued through its gravel lining. We sat
for a while admiring it.

'Ye won't get watther clearer than that anywhere,' said Frank admir-
ingly, as if it was all his own work. He filled the kettle and we strolled
back in leisurely fashion to the fire.

'The heather,' I remarked, 'has dried very quickly.'

'Ah, well, it wud,' said Frank knowledgeably. 'It doesn't houl' the
watther, an' with the sun an' a breeze it's as dry as snuff in a minute or
two.'

Our fire seemed to have grown in the half-hour since we had left it
and a sudden dread seized me.

'Frank,' I said in some alarm, 'I think our fire has spread.'

'Razus!' yodelled Frank, 'Connolly's coat,' and he leaped up on the
bank, followed more sedately by me. A patch of heather about six feet
square was still smouldering and right in the centre of it lay Connolly's
go-to-meetin' coat. More precisely, the four metal buttons and the
buckle of the belt lay in their correct positions on a coat-shaped
cobweb of ashes. A tentative thrust of my foot and it all disintegrated.

'Connolly won't like that,' I said.

'Connolly won't know,' Frank replied. 'He has more coats than
enough.' He picked up the buttons and the buckle and hurled them
in all directions across the bog. A few scuffling movements of his boots
and nothing but charred heather remained to mark his futile foray into
the dry-cleaning business.

When Connolly arrived back we were taking our ease with mugs of
tea in hand.

'Well, men,' he asked. 'What's the turf like?'

They were as wet, Frank informed him, as a certain plentiful farmyard commodity.

'We might as well gather up an' go home then,' said Connolly
resignedly, and turned back to the van.

'I needn't have bothered with this,' he called out and held up
Frank's battered old raincoat. 'Ye're a right eedjit headin' off to the

56

turf without a coat.'

'Ach dammit,' said Frank, getting into the passenger seat and winking at me, 'fellas goin' about in cars and vans don't need coats.'

'Ye're right there,' said Connolly, unaware of his loss and seemingly likely to remain so, 'there's nothin' ruins a good coat so quick.'

The Show

Schools in the country, for some unaccountable reason, used to be considered fair game for something euphemistically called The Show. Furtive and scruffy individuals were prone to appear unexpectedly and offer to 'do a show'. I never heard of any of them actually appearing twice at any one venue, a sinister enough thing in itself, but I don't necessarily agree with those cynics who suggest that they were devoured by an infuriated audience in some remote school in Tyrone. It is equally unlikely that they decamped for foreign parts with the tanners they collected. They were a mysterious breed, but the only truly magical thing about them was the way they materialised and de-materialised. No one ever saw them arrive, no one saw them go. Their gift was to manifest themselves and disappear before the row started.

They had much in common, these nomadic artists. If male, their white shirts proved to be grimy and ragged on closer inspection. If female, heavy make-up disguised the ravages of time and dissipation. Down-at-heel shoes and B.O. were almost regulation. Just why they chose to offer their services to schools I have never been able to fathom. Children are notoriously hard to entertain. Their minds are uncomplicated by the niceties of musical and dramatic appreciation, and country children, for all their airs of amiable innocence, can spot a phoney at a range of five hundred yards. Adults are inclined to give a fool a pardon but children are merciless. These wandering minstrels had a strong masochistic streak.

My first encounter with one of these entertainers was in the school corridor.

'Are you coming to the show?' boomed a voice from among the coat-racks as I passed and I leaped for the ceiling. Coming back to earth again I ventured among the forest of coats and found a female with a foot on a chair endeavouring to tie her plimsoll with a piece of binder twine. She straightened up and offered me a dazzling smile. At least it would have been dazzling had she possessed all her teeth. She was small, pear-shaped from the neck down, with a GI style haircut and a gingham dress that would have been better, much better, not belted.

'What show?' I asked politely, smothering a ludicrous image that sprang to mind. Females in cloakrooms offering to do a show reminded me of tales I had heard on the building sites in England, but we were in the heart of moral and rural Ulster, so I composed my features into an attentive mould.

'We're doing a show for the children here tomorrow,' she announced in a rumbling bass and advanced towards me waving one hand in the air. At this signal another female emerged from behind another coat-rack. This apparition was tall and straight, her hair was long and straight and she had the deadest face I have ever seen outside of a coffin.

'The headmaster says it's all right,' added the pear-shaped one. 'Isn't that so?' she went on, addressing the other one, who appeared to be deaf. The tall one's shoulders sagged, her knees sagged, but no flicker of expression indicated life. I formed the impression, though on what slender evidence I couldn't be sure, that they were a mother and daughter team.

'We'll see you tomorrow,' brayed the short one and clumped off towards the door. It's difficult to clump in plimsolls, but she managed it. The tall one followed, moving neither arms nor shoulders, but in total silence.

I went into the principal's room.

'Who are they?' I asked.

'I don't know their names,' he laughed. 'Let's just call them the Long and the Short of it.'

I looked out of the window to see what manner of transport they had but there was no sign of them. In the manner of their kind they had simply evaporated.

'How did they get here?' I asked mystified.

'By broomstick possibly,' the principal said. 'They sing a bit, play a guitar, do tricks and sketches. All for a tanner. In your room, to-morrow.'

I found myself viewing the morrow with some foreboding. Country children and their tanners were good close friends. Just how these two could produce enough entertainment to prevent themselves from being lynched was more than I could figure out just then.

The next morning my class and I were banished to the playground after roll-call. The Long and the Short needed the room to prepare for the spectacle. There was no difficulty about seeing into the room from the playground but there was nothing to be seen, much to the disappointment of the pupils who were having a desultory game of football. It's hard to concentrate on the game when all your instincts demand that you should be peering in at the window.

The performers had strung a curtain diagonally across one corner of the room and the preparations went on behind this. From time to time one of them emerged from behind the curtain and left the room. In the case of the Short, the journeys to the door were accompanied by expansive waving and much exposure of gums to the lacklustre footballers. The Long accomplished her travels without moving her shoulders and maintaining a deadpan expression. This gave rise to the speculation that she had been borrowed from the window of the local drapery shop and moved about on wee wheels.

In the fullness of time we were admitted to the presence. The Short collected the money at the door but when we entered the room it was to find that nothing had changed, nothing at all. The curtain was gone and the Long and the Short were the same as they had been the day before. I could sense disappointment in the audience. After such lengthy and mysterious preparations they had plainly expected costumes and magic. They had got desks and a blackboard.

'What were they doin' behind the curtain?' one of the girls asked loudly.

'They were shavin',' offered a senior boy, and sure enough one of them had acquired a number of reddish scratches on one cheek. Obviously the scratches were the result of attempting to apply grease-paint and giving it up as a bad job.

The Short was perched on the front of my desk. She smiled at the audience but her shortage of teeth made the effect more menacing than welcoming. The Long sat on my chair beside the desk, her hands folded in her lap and her customary blank expression firmly lodged in place. The Short had a guitar wedged between thigh and elbow.

'Would you like me to sing a song?' she grated.

There was no reply. Had she been able to judge the mood of incipient mutiny in her audience, she would have given them their money back and left there and then. As it was, they merely stared back in silent hostility.

'All right,' she continued gaily, 'I'll sing you a song.'

This piece of effrontery drew some shuffling of feet. The audience didn't realise they had been asked a rhetorical question. They thought they had been offered a choice, they had voted for silence and were being denied their democratic rights.

She announced that she would sing them a cowboy song. The boys at least brightened a bit at this, for they were Western fans, thronging the village cinema's Saturday afternoon performance as often as they could escape their farmyards and their parents' conviction that the cinema was a short-cut to damnation.

The Short couldn't sing. She couldn't do much with the guitar either. The Long didn't offer to do anything at all. She merely sat like the spectre at the feast staring at the audience. The Short struggled manfully with her ballad. It appeared that a cowboy had come to town and there he had committed some misdemeanour or other, she snarled at the audience.

'Then came a big policeman and took him down and he's in the jail-house now, ha ha ha, he he he, ho ho ho,' she screamed at them.

Now every child in that audience knew that Western towns didn't have policemen. They had sheriffs. They turned to each other and announced this fact.

A more intelligent performer would have taken diversionary action but not the Short. The ha-ha-ha he-he-he ho-ho-ho of this obviously homemade song was accompanied by a dramatic gesture which consisted of pointing at a member of the audience. If this was meant to represent some kind of primitive, nominal audience involvement, the effect was somewhat different. The nicotine-stained finger was duly levelled at Big Brian and he was ha-ha-ha-ed at. The rest of the audience, bored stiff by the performance so far, joined with gusto in the ha-ha-ing and the pointing. Brian, an affable, easygoing lad, tolerated it the first time, blushing to the roots of his hair. When it happened a second time, he got off the cupboard he was perched on and offered, as he put it rather elegantly, to scatter anyone who so much as looked at him. He didn't specifically exclude the singer from this threat, so she abandoned the cowboy to the tender mercies of his Western jailers and hurriedly offered to do some tricks. The principal, seated in the front row, half rose and quelled the audience with his lethal eyebrow. Silence descended. I had the feeling that, as a local expression had it, there would be harm done and people hurted when the performers departed.

The singing had merely been bad. The magic was abysmal. Long took no part in this either, but as the Short turned her back on the audience to make preparations for her conjuring, the Long yawned. It was a splendid yawn and the audience watched in total fascination as she displayed tongue, tonsils and dental fillings lengthily and luxuriously. When she finally closed her mouth, some of the toddlers in the front clapped enthusiastically. The bigger children laughed uproariously at this gaffe, pounding each other on the back and guffawing with totally unnecessary volume. The principal had recourse to his eyebrow again and peace descended.

The magic turn began with that ancient nursery rhyme about two little blackbirds, improbably named Peter and Paul. The audience groaned at this wane's stuff, as one of them muttered darkly. Their wrath turned to glee when the pieces of paper that represented the birds fell, unnoticed by the performer, so that when she sought triumphantly to make the birds reappear, she held up two bare fingers. The audience howled with monstrous joy.

Card tricks were next. The Short had first to conceal the cards up her sleeves and she turned her back to perform this essential operation. As she turned back the cards fell like confetti from her sleeves and the audience cheered with delight. The principal rose like the wrath of God but before he could speak, the door opened and the clerical manager thrust his head into the room. The principal joined him in the corridor and as the door closed behind him a voice said to me, 'Please, Sir, may I leave the room?'

It was one of the senior girls and there was the merest twitch at the corner of her mouth. Now all teachers who atone for their sins by supervising school entertainments know that once the audience begins to trickle out to the toilet, it's time to ring down the curtain. I looked towards the front of the room. The Short looked uncertainly at me. Then I noticed Peter looking at me. Peter was a remarkably angelic-looking twelve-year-old and many a one before, and no doubt since, has been taken in by his expression.

'Please Sir,' he said, 'if we gave them another tanner wud they stop?'

They stopped for free and without so much as a final handclap the audience stamped out of the room and into the playground. I made signs to indicate that I would inform the principal that the show was over and fled to his room. He was sitting at his desk and I fancied I could see smoke coming from his ears.

'Are they away?' he asked hopefully.

'No, but they're folding their tents,' I told him. He looked at me dully.

'I must go and ah...speak to them,' he announced and drifted off down the corridor. He was back in a second or two, mystified.

'There's not a sign of them,' he said. 'Thank God,' he added fervently.

I was supervising the cloakrooms that evening and the last one out was Anthony, the present representative of a long line of hill farmers.

'What did you think of the show, Anthony?' I asked, poker-faced. He tilted his head to one side and made a pattern on the floor with the toe of his shoe. Had he been a few years older, he would, I felt certain, have spat thoughtfully. Then this little man, with the wisdom of ages in his eyes gave me a sidelong look.

'It was nothin' but an oul' catchpenny,' he said. As he turned away, he added over his shoulder, 'Sir.'

Eavesdropping

Mr Mick Millan was a power in the land when I began my teaching career. He would have been flattered, I'm sure, to know that he had an admirer in the foothills of the Sperrins, even if she was only ten years old and rendered his major utterances in the most ragged of prose in her diary. I learned much about many things from the diaries of Deirdre and her classmates, for the diary was my devious, if somewhat unethical, way of building up my background knowledge of the community I taught in. I issued everyone with an exercise book labelled 'Diary' and invited them to write down their thoughts on anything or anybody that had aroused their interest in the previous twenty-four hours. It was not, I assured them grandly, to be regarded as any kind of English exercise. No inquisitions would be held into the niceties of grammar or spelling, nothing would be formally marked or corrected. For fifteen minutes every day they could do their own thing, without let or hindrance.

They went to work with a will and showered me with masses of information on the locality, much of it possibly libellous. Certainly had some unscrupulous reporter from the more sensational Sunday papers read some of the information recorded in the diaries, he would have pricked up his ear in joyful anticipation. I was astonished at the wide range of interest of my charges, for they wrote on every subject under the sun. After a while, Deirdre's fascination for the political career of Mr Mick Millan, British Prime Minister of 'You've-never-had-it-so-good' fame began to seem quite commonplace.

One day I was jolted into scandalised alertness to learn that Father Halligan, our amiable local curate, had been out with Sweet Lips the night before. In those days clerical celibacy was taken for granted so the laconic reference to Father Halligan's nocturnal activities rocked me more than somewhat. Besides, I was a little disappointed to find out that there was a siren popularly know as Sweet Lips in the district and I was the last to hear of her propensities. The mystery was cleared up just before lunch-time when the clerical renegade breezed cheerfully into the school with a sally rod under his arm and a look of carefully assumed innocence on his face.

My brief acquaintance with him had taught me that he was an extrovert character with a passion for music of all types and a hilarious line in yarns...but some maiden called Sweet Lips...?

'Do you know, Master,' he said with pseudo-grimness, 'some of these villains of yours were tramping through my garden last night. I've told them if they leave any more hoofprints in my rosebeds I'll take a stick to them. Isn't that right boys?'

The culprits, grinning widely, agreed that this was so. They knew there was about as much chance of his taking his stick to them as setting them on fire. He made a sweeping motion of the sally rod through the air and they listened in mock fright to its swishing sound.

'So there you are,' he told them solemnly. 'This is Sweet Lips and that's her song. You'll hear it and feel it if you don't stay out of my roses. Morning children,' 'Morning Master,' and off he went singing a current popular song, 'Put your sweet lips a little closer to the phone.'

My experience of the Sweet Lips incident fortunately prepared me for another cryptic entry a few days later. 'Daddy was in Derry with the woman yesterday,' it read but I already knew that the word 'woman' could be invested with many shades of meaning. Thus if someone said he saw Joe Murphy out with 'the woman' yesterday, Joe was a bachelor and 'the woman' his fiancee. Had Joe, on the other hand, been seen out with 'his woman', she would have been his wife. The possibility of their being out together, however, was remote, unless it was a wedding, a funeral or a christening. Woman's place was restricted to the home, the background or the wrong. Once a girl started to go steady, she degenerated from having a name of her own to being 'the woman'. If she persisted in her foolhardy ways and married the fellow, she was 'his woman'. This erosion of identity, however, deterred few girls from the matrimonial stakes as far as I could see.

In this case 'the woman' was not Daddy's girlfriend, for his wife would have permitted no such luxury. In a certain tone of voice, or in a certain context, 'the woman' was a lady official of some kind. In this instance Daddy had been involved in an accident and was on crutches and she had chauffeured him to Derry on some business concerning compensation.

She was one of a profession then in its infancy, and to some of the locals, unaccustomed to the burgeoning jargon of the welfare state, she was 'the wee farewell lady'! Even I could work that one out. She was a welfare worker.

Milestones on the road to socially acceptable behaviour were duly recorded in the diaries. 'It is a good manner to say excuse me when you make a noise you didn't want to make,' I learned from one lad. Well, discordant noises issue from both ends of undisciplined bodies and one mother had apparently decided enough was enough.

For several days in succession I tried in vain to interpret one illegible scrawl, in which I could recognise only one word. With Sweet Lips and 'the woman' safely behind me, however, 'wench' gave me little cause for concern. After a week of 'wenches' however, my curiosity could no longer be contained.

'Martin,' I said, choosing my words with care, 'do you know what a wench is?'

He gave me a pitying, sure-everybody-know-that kind of look. 'A wench,' he informed me loftily, 'is for pickin' up.'

Sweet Lips and 'the woman' had not been enough to complete my apprenticeship, I thought, debating whether to continue the conversation. I decided to brazen this one out. You never know, I reasoned, there just might be the makings of a sex-maniac in my class.

'For picking up what?' I demanded, aware that I was breaking my rule not to hold inquisitions.

'Anythin',' he replied, patiently. 'Heavy things, mostly.' He thought hard, a furrow of concentration on his brow as he sought to find words simple enough to educate this idiot teacher, then he brightened.

'Ye can pull tree stumps out of the ground with them,' he added, triumphantly.

All was well. The lad, obviously of a mechanical turn of mind, filled his days and nights with thoughts of winches.

A farmer whose cornfield adjoined the local football field had developed a somewhat acrimonious relationship with the boys in my class, as a result of their frequent forays into his crop in pursuit of stray footballs. Bad news travels with extraordinary rapidity in the country and several pupils reported in graphic detail a near accident he had while crossing a ditch with a loaded shotgun in pursuit of a marauding fox. As I read one account of the incident I took a thoughtful look at the author's face but there was nothing in his innocent expression to suggest that the substitution of an *i* for an *o* in 'nearly shot himself' was anything but the oversight it appeared to be. Still, I wondered...

A weak, I discovered, was what kept a bedroom lamp lit and a kennel was something you lit a fire with. Obviously the local dog population did not live in very sophisticated surroundings. Kathleen, a good-living child, apparently considered that I was in need of spiritual enlightenment and brightened many a dull Monday morning with a detailed account of Sunday's sermon. From her I learned that one of the ten lepers was a smart man and that Simon Sweeney, a somewhat belligerent local tramp, had apparently been reincarnated. He had, she informed me via her diary, assisted Our Lord to carry the cross. I gathered a rich harvest that morning, for it had been a very windy Sunday and a gust had carried her hat away. All ended well, however, for she had run smartly after it and found it in a poodle.

The same wind had carried away part of the roof of a house and one diarist had recorded that you could see the laughter. I bent my no-comment rule once again to mention that there was nothing funny about losing a roof.

'But Sir,' he protested, much hurt, 'the laughters is what the slates is nailed till.'

The class fell about laughing at this appalling display of ignorance and the young author veered between tears and murder.

'It is not, Sir,' howled one lad in helpless mirth. 'A laughter is where ye keep hay or corn.'

Most of the farm byres in the district were two-storey affairs, with the cow-stalls on the ground floor, and the second floor, reached by an external flight of stone steps, was used for storing sacks of corn and a reserve supply of hay for winter feeding of the downstairs residents. A loft, in short, corrupted locally to 'laft'.

Some entries were decidedly mysterious. 'He was off for a few days but after a litter he soon got better.' read a fascinating one-sentence statement. I pondered that for a good while but decided not to investigate it. It could turn out to be something simple, like a misplaced pronoun or adjective, or just a misspelling, that seemed to upset the laws of biology. On the other hand it could be something well outside my comprehension, so I left well alone, I also refused to rise to the bait proffered by another diarist's one-line entry. 'You can do another thing on a table.' A fellow fresh from the building sites of England has heard, if not always believed, all about the more exotic table-top sports. Probing could lead to yet another anticlimax, but on the other hand, you never could be sure.

In more prosaic vein, one avid reader of *Old Moore's Almanac* filled a newsless day by informing his diary that there would be an earclips on the sun on the fifteenth and his mother had apparently balanced the household budget by selling some hens to the poultry dealer. The poultry dealer, who went round the farms in a van buying up surplus hens, ducks and even geese was known locally as the fowl-man, except to my pupil who wrote him down as 'foul man'. The dealer was a pleasant character in fact, and I often met him, but I smothered the temptation to mention this episode to him. There is a limit, after all, to the liberties you can take with a fellow who wrings dozens of necks every day as a matter of course.

'Please Sir,' asked one bright young lady one morning, 'can you write poetry in your diary?'

'Of course,' I replied in delight. My teaching was bearing fruit. Self-expression was paying off. My moment of self-delusion soon passed, for what I got was the first verse of 'The Ballad of Father Gilligan', with an accidental amendment the poet would not have appreciated.

> 'The old priest Peter Gilligan,' I read,
> 'Was weary night and day,
> For half his flock were in his bed,
> Or under green sods lay.'

Well I suppose that would explain his weariness all right.

'Malcolm calls the bore Barney,' I read on another apparently newsless day.

'Who's Barney?' I asked conversationally, intending to avoid his company.

'A he-pig,' was the laconic reply.

Some pupils, freed from the restrictions imposed by formal English lessons and essay-writing exercises, experimented with ideas and words they would not have normally used, but experience soon taught me that much of what was written was in fact snatches of adult conversation, wrongly heard or imperfectly understood. One youngster's lengthy but unintelligible entry concluded with the startling statement,

68

'A midwife is a person who looks on the dark side of things.' I chewed my pencil over that one and failed to come up with any enlightenment.

'A person who looks on the dark side of things,' I whispered confidentially to the author, 'is a pessimist, not a midwife.'

'No Sir,' he whispered back in a not-an-inch voice, 'a midwife looks on the dark side of things.'

I tried this one out on the district nurse and she thought it hilarious. 'I can't explain it,' she laughed, 'but more than once I've delivered babies on these hillsides and the only light was from the headlights of my car shining through the window.'

As time went on, the increasing frequency of one-line entries, intriguing and enlightening though many of them were, made me feel that my grand plan for building up background knowledge through literary licence was beginning to wilt slightly at the edges. I decided to end the experiment but was forced to wait a while lest my action should appear to be mere pique. The entry that compelled this delay occurred the Monday morning I arrived in school wearing a new suit. Kathleen eyed me critically and forswearing the usual ration of spiritual enlightenment for her dear teacher, commented on the suit instead. She always spoke at breathless speed and conveyed the same quality to her writing by omitting anything remotely resembling punctuation.

'The Master has a new suit it is awful,' was her hasty comment.

Well, as my grandmother used to say, eavesdroppers never hear anything good about themselves.

Heresy!

There is nothing in my experience that quite compares with the Religious Examination as administered in the Fifties. Veterans have assured me that it was kids' stuff when compared to the inquisitions they used to suffer in earlier decades, and I have nodded non-committally. My own feeling was that the Inquisition itself would have cheerfully surrendered its ancient equivalent of red-hot barbed-wire in exchange for a crash course in the now long defunct system.

It was not simply a test of theoretical religion as far as the pupils were concerned but a question of professional survival for the teachers. The examination didn't seek to establish what the children knew, but what they didn't know. The area of ignorance was held to be in direct proportion to the competence, conviction or aetheism of the teacher. The significance of the exam lay in the fact that by the Fifties, the increasing complexity of the educational system and the growing influence of the teachers' unions meant that the only area where clerical management held undisputed control was in the sphere of the religious examination. Where the Ministry Inspector sought merely to assess, generally in a courteous manner, the professional competence of the teacher and his worth to the tax-paying public (a controversial enough point in itself) the Ecclesiastical Inspector sought to establish to what extent the public needed protection from the evil machinations of the secular and licentious teaching profession.

The teacher, of course, sought to refute this innuendo by deeds, not words. He endeavoured to cover the extensive religious course so that his charges would answer without fail the cunning questions the E.I. would pose. It mattered nothing that most of the teaching was beyond the comprehension of many of the pupils, for the curriculum made no concessions to those who were not too bright or had poor memories; if they could answer parrot-fashion all would be well.

Thus, in the dark days of the winter term, you might encounter strong men (and women) huddled in groups and hear strange snatches of conversation such as 'I hear when he was up in Tirboy he was asking about...' and whatever the topic was it was sure to produce a strangled cry of 'Oh, my God, I haven't done that with my class.' This piteous wail was delivered in the tones of a man who has arrived home to find the house burning and then realises that the money he has spent with such abandon in the pub was the fire premium.

As the E.I. and his retinue closed in on the school, the teacher's efforts grew more frantic. He knew what had been asked in other schools, for his free time was devoted to interrogating their staffs, and he tried to think like an examiner. Would he ask the same topics twice or find new angles on an old one? Why all the panic, you may ask. Well, there was The Report, a booklet which listed all the schools by name and class. The grades, which ranged from Excellent down to Fair, were listed against each class. Thus every teacher, and everyone else who cared to look, could see everyone else's marks, and to get anything less than Excellent as far as some managers were concerned meant that a kind of spiritual police action was required by a missionary commando. More important by far was the fact that if one was eventually seeking appointment as a principal, a mere 'Very Good' in a Report was tantamount to perpetual banishment from the higher echelons of one's profession.

So I approached my first examination in much the same spirit as the Early Christians faced the lions, only less so. From all I had heard, the Christians had some chance of winning. Shortly after the appointed time, the E.I. arrived, accompanied by the clerical manager and the curate. The E.I. settled himself at my desk and opened the proceedings with a quick joke or two, at which the pupils politely bared their teeth. The manager stationed himself in a commanding position, leaned forward and brooded ominously. The curate tried to make himself invisible at the back of the room.

The E.I., I discovered, had an impressive conjuring trick. He had a a list of the pupils in exactly the same order as the roll-book and opposite each name was a line of squares, the whole thing rather like a football coupon. A quick check of the roll-book showed that no one was absent. No one would dare be absent on the day of the examination. Failure to attend would definitely be regarded as a hanging offence.

The E.I. then handed me back the roll-book and proceeded with the examination, calling out each name in turn from his list. I could see that the pupils were baffled by this stranger who seemed to know their names without the help of the roll-book. I too was somewhat baffled as to how he had acquired the list, but the psychological advantage this trick gave him was impressive. The children, mini-cynics though they might be, were made to see that he was no ordinary mortal.

The examination proceeded uneventfully. Little voices trotted out answers with admirable, if mechanical fervour. One or two minor wrong answers were given, but on the whole I was well satisfied with the performance and I was beginning to think that the gruesome tales my veteran colleagues had been telling me were all a gigantic leg-pull. Then the axe fell, neatly shearing off any chance I might ever have had of becoming a principal in that district.

'Tell me, Margaret, can you say Grace before meals?' asked the E.I. without lifting his head from the list. Margaret sprang to her feet and delivered the prayer in one unintelligible breath. 'Very good indeed, indeed, Margaret,' said the E.I. with deceptive cheerfulness. 'Now one last question and I'll be finished. Can anyone, anyone at all, tell me why we say Grace before meals?'

Now the children knew their Grace, they knew the drill, but no one can do everything, and it had never occured to me in my inexperience to treat the prayer as anything other than self-explanatory. The response to the question was stony silence, punctuated, appropriately enough, by a rumbling stomach. The manager frowned ominously and the E.I's cheerful smile began to fade. Then to my horror Andy rose to his feet. Andy, whose education was currently running at a staggering four bathroom windows a year, Andy who never volunteered an answer for the perfectly adequate reason that he knew none, was now offering one.

'Well, Andrew,' said the E.I. without recourse to his list, for it was no great trick to remember a lad of such build, 'why do we say Grace before meals?'

Andy braced himself, threw back his shoulders and gave me an I'll-show-ye look. Then he addressed the E.I.

'For fear ye'd be choked,' he informed him smugly.

I could see Andy's point, for the lad was of an aggressive turn of mind and his primitive memory retained some fragments of stories about a wrathful God punishing his disobedient people with fire and flood. Such a God, reasoned the young troglodyte, would think nothing of blocking the gullet of an ungrateful diner. The E.I. was not devoid of humour and he nodded and smiled but made no comment.

Then a chair scraped back and the clerical manager stalked majestic-ally towards the door, With one hand on the handle he turned and beckoned me out. I followed him into the corridor.

'So,' he growled, 'that's what you're teaching them, is it?'

'What?' I asked innocently.

'Heresy!' he thundered. 'That's what. Heresy!'

'Considering,' I said carefully, 'the nature of the question, and the difficulty of anticipating everything the examiner...'

'Don't,' he ordered me grimly, 'dare to criticise the examiner. You're a member of the union, no doubt.'

I admitted this and he nodded triumphantly.

'Communists!' he snapped. 'They're all communists!'

He turned on his heel and made his way towards the principal's room, leaving me struggling with the desire to go back and administer to Andy the fate he felt awaited Graceless diners. As it turned out, when the report eventually came, the class was graded as Excellent. Too late to do me any good, though, for by then in the quarters that mattered I was marked down as the man who believed that Grace before meals was a cross between insurance and blackmail.

The lives of rural teachers were complicated by more than E.I.s. They at least came only once a year. The Ministry of Education appeared, on the surface at least, a good deal less trusting, for their inspectors arrived much more frequently and, unlike the E.I., invariably without warning. A favourite time with some of them was either two minutes after school started or two minutes before it finished, in the fond hope of catching teachers arriving late or leaving early. Life was a constant battle of wits between these two sides, but unlike the E.I.s, the teachers had a chance of winning occasionally in a confrontation with the Ministry's officials.

I had no dramatic confrontations with Ministry inspectors during my stay in the school, but I nearly set one on fire, something which made me rather unpopular with some of my colleague who would rather I had succeeded. This particular official had earned a good deal of unpopularity around the district for his underhand activities. An ex-service officer, he firmly believed that everyone was up to something, and the fact that he never actually caught anybody seemed to disappoint him a good deal. On one occasion he intercepted a note in transit between two schools and delivered it in person. There were eight schools in the area, some of them quite close together and when the inspector appeared at one of them one day, the principal dispatched a boy with a note to the next school to warn the head teacher there. The inspector, watching for something of the sort, suddenly excused himself and hurried after the boy in his car. When he caught up with him he told the boy to go back to school and that he would deliver the note personally.

When he arrived at the next school he simply handed the note to the principal and waited for a result. The note bore the single word 'Inspector'.

'But why did you write it down?' asked the principal in pseudo-amazement. 'I know you're an inspector.'

My own unwitting attempt to set the same gentleman on fire arose partly because of his devious habit of parking his car some distance from the school and approaching on foot. My class were writing an essay and I had taken advantage of the industrious quiet to nip across to the staff-room for a quiet smoke. I had just finished the cigarette, but instead of stubbing out the butt on an ashtray as a normal person would have done, I dropped it, still smouldering, out of the open window. The staff-room window was rather high and when I looked out to see where the cigarette had gone, I was just in time to see it travelling towards the front door of the school on the hat of a man moving bent over double. It was our man, making a cautious and hopeful approach. I peered from behind the staff-room door as he tiptoed down the corridor, with a wisp of smoke rising from the hat. At the door of the principal's room — to my vast relief — he removed the hat and the smouldering butt fell to the floor. Hastily I disposed of the evidence.

'He'll be wondering,' I said to the principal later, 'where the burn mark came from.'

'It's a pity,' the principal answered, 'that it hadn't burned a nice little round hole. He'd wonder a great deal more about that.'

The school nearest to ours was under the command of a somewhat past middleage spinster. She was a trifle eccentric about time-keeping and this fact was duly reported to the Ministry by someone or other in the locality who didn't wish her well. This well-wisher didn't, however, mention that her eccentricity was as likely to take the form of her arriving long before school started and staying on late, or indeed that her disregard for time was more than amply compensated for by the excellence of her teaching. Our inspector arrived one morning before nine o'clock hoping to find the school unopened. The lady, however, was at her desk engrossed in her paper-work and she made no comment about his early arrival. Acting on the principle that she wouldn't expect lightning to strike twice, he arrived somewhat earlier the next morning and found her marking essays. She viewed him with some distaste.

'I don't mind you coming in so early,' she informed him icily, 'but you should realise that if it continues, the people around here will be wondering just what the two of us are up to alone in the school.'

I'm sure it was just coincidence that a new inspector arrived shortly after this, but as we toasted the quick-thinking lady when the news got out we preferred to think it was her doing.

Friendly Advice

I was leaning on the parapet of the bridge one day after school, chin in hands, listening to the water trickling over the stones and thinking of nothing in particular. I was in that comfortable state of suspended animation known as a brown study when I noticed that a black boot had appeared on the grass verge and as I reluctantly moved my head to investigate this phenomenon I realised that the boot was on a foot projecting from a bottle-green trouser-leg and that I had been joined by the local police sergeant. He had crept up on a Velocette, a notoriously silent motor-cycle much favoured by the police in those days.

'It's a grand day, he said. 'A grand day for leaning on the bridge and looking at nothing in particular.'

'Just what I was doing,' I replied and added, rather pointedly, 'That's a very silent machine you have there.'

'It's a great machine, sure enough,' said the sergeant affably, viewing the grey monster with affection. 'It beats the old three-speed push-bike any day. Man dear, you could hear the ticking of the old three-speeds for miles on a quiet day.'

He removed his crash-helmet, placed it carefully on the wall, took a packet of Players from his tunic pocket and offered me one. We smoked in silence for a while.

'They say,' he said at length, 'that just round the bend of the river ther, just over the bank, there's a well with a trout in it that's seven years old.'

'I heard about that,' I said cautiously. I was acquiring the traditional rural reticence in dealing with strangers, especially those in uniform.

'It's nearly all head now, I believe,' he went on. 'They say that's what happens. The head just gets bigger and bigger till it dies.'

'I've heard of something to that effect,' I said, just to keep the conversation going. The big-headed trout was the pride and joy of one of my pupils on whose father's land the well was situated. In the one-man-upmanship stakes it left the bird's-nest experts in the halfpenny place.

'I wonder,' the sergeant said speculatively, 'how it got into the well?'

'It's a local mystery,' I agreed.

'Do you fish at all?' he asked, flicking his cigarette butt into the river and closely watching it float out of sight under the arch.

'Not a lot,' I admitted. This was not strictly true, but in view of my total ignorance of local angling regulations and permits, I was prepared to forgo any proof of sterling character that the sport might bestow. We silently viewed the water for a while.

'I don't suppose,' the sergeant said at length, 'you've ever heard of Master Loughlin?'

'The name sounds familiar,' I said noncommittally. The sergeant laughed. Everyone had heard of Loughlin and his band of bachelor brothers. They were a law unto themselves in the valley where they lived.

'A desperate man,' said the sergeant, shaking his head. 'I was stationed up there before I came here.'

He settled himself more comfortably on his elbows and studied the river with profound interest. There was a local legend of Loughlin being pursued across several miles of mountain roads with a bagful of illicit salmon, a delicacy for which he and the rest of the district had a decided weakness. His brothers, so the story went, for it lost little in the telling, had bought time for him by the strategic use of broken glass which had brought the police car to a halt with a flat tyre. By the time the law caught up with him he was dozing by his fire in suspiciously dry clothing, but of the salmon there was no sign.

'You know,' the sergeant went on reflectively, 'one of his brothers was heavily fined for making poteen a few years back. My predecessor caught him. Had to, there was an official complaint. But you've heard the story, I'm sure.'

77

I had. The local version was that the wily and devil-may-care Loughlin had retrieved virtually all the confiscated liquor. The waste pipe from that particular station kitchen led into a stream at a spot which could not be seen from inside. Loughlin, armed with suitable containers, had taken up position under cover of darkness. When justice took its course and the poteen, save for the sample required by law, was poured down the sink, Loughlin had simply collected it and its subsequent sale paid the brother's fine, no doubt with something over for expenses.

'A very clever man,' said the sergeant thoughtfully. 'B.A. and all that. They think the world of him up there. But it's a pity too, in a way. A fellow with all that intelligence just spending his life as principal of a two-teacher school out in the bogs.'

Just the right place for him, argued many of his more sedate colleagues. A man like him, with or without his brothers, they reasoned, would provide serious competition for the Mafia in a city. I kept this comment to myself. Besides, I had an uneasy feeling that I knew where this conversation was leading.

'You don't like,' said the sergeant, looking up at the sky and focussing intently on a passing crow, 'to be making trouble for people. Around here, now, there's no real crime. Bikes without lights is about the most serious offence you come across. And there's after-hours drinking, of course, not that that's a terribly serious thing either.'

He flashed the cigarettes again.

'Well, I mean to say, it's a farming community and the men work all the daylight hours at the hay and the turf and so forth, and what with feeding the calves and milking the cows after that, sure it's practically bedtime before they have a chance to go and have a bottle of stout.'

I solemnly nodded agreement to these sentiments and inwardly cursed Donovan, for he was the root cause of this roundabout conversation.

'Of course,' the sergeant went on, speaking to the end of his cigarette, 'it gets abused, drinking after hours. There's fellows that finish their day's work early and they have no real call to be sitting in pubs till the middle of the night.'

'It should be kept for the farmers,' I offered tentatively.

The sergeant eyed me blandly.

'Exactly,' he said. 'That's more or less the way we look at it. Your average farmer, now, he drinks a bottle or maybe two, no more, and yarns with his neighbours about cattle prices. They don't get full and drive motors recklessly or anything like that, so there's no real harm done by anybody. But y'see, there's complaints, and sometimes they're made high up and we have to take action.'

The sergeant, for all his affability, was not going to end his career as a village policeman.

'Now there was a man recently,' he went on, 'and he went into a local pub on a payday and he stayed there till he had disposed of his pay-packet. Now that's irresponsible, that's wrong. His wife wrote to the D.I. and he was round in a flash threatening blue murder. We had to raid the place. You follow me?'

Only too well, I thought and nodded sagely. It was no secret, for twelve people were booked that night, including two local teachers, but what made the headlines was the fact that the teachers, carefree bachelors both, had for devilment given wrong names to the police. The police knew them, of course, but the law had to go through the motions of formally identifying them, a fact that the magistrate had commented severely on. He also added a few strictures about the right of the public to expect responsible behaviour from men in their position.

'Well, there you have it, you see,' said the sergeant regretfully. 'A thing like that looks bad on a man's record, maybe when he's going after a bigger school or something like that. Foolish, downright foolish.'

I flashed the cigarettes this time but the sergeant was incorruptible.

'Ah sure I smoke far too much,' he said, reaching for his crash helmet. 'I'm off. Must keep an eye on the flock, y'see.' The Velocette purred into life and the policeman eyed the gleaming toe of his boot.

'I enjoyed the wee yarn,' he said slowly. 'You'll mind what I was saying?'

'I'll do that, sergeant,' I said casually and he drifted silently away. I had been duly warned and I resolved to have a word or two with Donovan on the subject.

There was a carnival in progress at the time and the local imagination was rather limited as to what it should consist of, apart from lavish profits for the ever-hungry building fund, so there tended to be a disproportionate number of football matches and track events. Football matches had the merit of being easy to organise for they were little more than a thinly disguised form of hillbilly feuding. For partisan reasons they attracted large attendances, mostly from the feuding contenders of former years and their relations, anxious to perpetuate their grievances down into the twenty-first century and beyond. Donovan and I had repaired to one of these battles the previous evening.

Due to an extraordinary oversight on the part of one player who in a moment of weakness had concentrated on the game instead of the opposing team, a goal was scored. Donovan loudly applauded this achievement, a wrong move, I soon realised, for we were in the midst of the other side's supporters. They were wrathful. One of them, apparently carved from granite, leaned across me and addressed himself to Donovan.

'That,' he ordered brusquely, 'will be enough outta you, Donovan.'

'Bully Francie,' enthused Donovan, unaware that he had been ordered to desist.

'Donovan,' menaced the granite one, 'ye have relations in Tirboy. What are ye cheerin' him for?'

Donovan took his eyes from the game and viewed the Tirboy supporter up and down.

'I wud never,' he informed him, dangerously polite, 'let on in public that I had any connection wi' Tirboy. It is, savin' yer presence,' he nodded to me, 'the backside of nowhere at all. It's inhabited by a race of bloody bogmen that shud nivir have been let outta the caves they wur rared in. Gouttrels, the lotta them.'

He paused to consider the effect of this speech and was apparently dissatisfied.

'Is it true,' he asked, 'that ye ate yer mate raw up there still?'

The granite one swept me out of the way with one arm and lashed out at Donovan. Donovan moved a fraction and the Tirboy supporter skidded past, slipped and fell face down in the grass. It was a suitable resting place, for cows had recently been in possession of the field and left ample evidence of their passing.

'Stay where ye are,' ordered Donovan happily. 'Ye smell the same, stannin' or lyin'. Come on,' he said to me. 'We'll lave these bogmen to kill each other.'

Another Tirboy supporter blocked our path.

'That goal shuddn't a bin allowed,' he snarled. 'The Tirboy goalie…'

Donovan thrust his hands into his trousers pockets and looked at the man carefully.

'Ye take a fatherly interest in the Tirboy goalie, don't ye?' he said contemptuously and to my astonishment the Tirboy man cringed back grinning nervously. Donovan stalked off and I followed mystified.

'What was that about the goalie?' I asked as we got to the gate.

'That's his da,' said Donovan happily. 'I was nivir sure, but begod I know now. Some of these boyos aren't as holy as they make out.'

We clattered off in Donovan's Rover to a pub at the far side of the district. He let me know I would have to find my own way home, for his mission was to see the barmaid home. The place was full when we arrived. Donovan duly disappeared and I was ushered into the back kitchen, which was full of haymaking farmers relaxing. The only place I could find to stand was just against the door, a decidedly uncomfortable spot, for as people came and went I was propelled backwards and forwards with the edge of the door seemingly attached to my spine. The crack was good, for I knew some of the drinkers so transport home was assured, and the time flew. It was just about midnight and I was regaling the company with the story of the incident at the match when the door opened for the umpteenth time and I was once again propelled into the middle of the floor. Then the door gently closed again and I travelled back with it, never bothering to look round.

I kept on talking and I was developing some considerable regard for my powers as a raconteur, for the eyes of the company were rivetted on me in a way that seldom happened in school. As the door closed, one farmer let out a grateful sigh.

'That was the sergeant lookin' over yer shoulder, Master,' he croaked. 'Didn't ye see us signin' to ye?'

Glasses were downed in a flash and in seconds the place was empty, for everybody, including myself, was sure the policeman would have second thoughts, come back and book the lot of us. When we got outside, there was only Donovan's ancient Rover and the van I was getting a lift in to be seen. The policeman had vanished as mysteriously as he had arrived.

The day after my conversation with the sergeant, Donovan was sitting on the school wall when I came out.

'I hear ye've been assistin' the polis with their enquiries,' he announced.

'How did you know?' I demanded.

'Around here, if a blackbird lit on the Moss Road in the mornin' they'd know all about in the Sixtowns before dinnertime,' grinned Donovan. 'Well, what did the sergeant want with ye?'

'He was advising me to choose my company with greater care,' I told him gravely.

'Begod,' laughed Donovan, 'he's the man to advise right enough. He's not too particular who he's seen wi' if he's ready to stand on the roadside and talk to the likes of you.'

'As a matter of fact,' I informed him rather grandly, 'he was advising me on the danger to my career prospects of being found on licensed premises after hours. He even quoted a few examples.' Briefly I told him the whole story.

'Dammit,' said Donovan, 'that's the rarest good turn I ever heard of a schoolmaster doin' for anybody. Ye got the whole pubful off because he didn't want it on yer record. That's a lesson'll take some batin', so it will.'

'He seems a right sort of a fellow,' I remarked.

'Yer granny,' snorted Donovan derisively. 'He got me for no tax on the Rover on the way out.'

The Sobering of Barney Ned

Wee John McNally was, as the locals euphemistically put it, a bit odd. He was somewhat given to talking to himself, but that was only his way of having a sensible chat. Sometimes he would reply to a neighbourly greeting, sometimes he would simply shamble past with a sidelong glare at the speaker for interrupting his conversation. He never went anywhere without a wool-bale, a capacious and versatile sack used for the storing and transportation of fleeces. Everything John needed to transport he carried in the wool-bale, whether it was a few groceries, a supply of turf or an ailing sheep. Hung from his head like a hood and roped around the waist it did bad-weather duty as a cloak. He was by profession a sheepfarmer in a small way of business but by inclination he was a breeder of sheepdogs, a vocation at which he excelled. A sheepdog reared from a pup of John's was the best there was in two counties. Although farmers would have paid any price for a pup of John's they couldn't always get one. Sometimes he would sell one, sometimes he would give one away. At other times he would blandly assert that there wasn't a dog about the place, even though he was at that moment standing in the midst of a howling multitude of them. It was a matter of how you took him, the locals said enigmatically. Occasionally when the dog population threatened to engulf him completely he would carry out a culling operation by drowning pups and even half-grown dogs in the pool below the stepping stones.

A mile away on the other side of the valley lived John's mother. While the locals dismissed John as merely a bit odd, they described Jane as being as odd as tay. Wee, wizened, widowed and waspish, she lived in a storey-and-half dwelling in the midst of tiny fields that seemed to stand on their ends. The cattle she grazed in them must have had suction cups for hooves, and they were thoroughly spoiled. She fed them on everything edible until they were as fat as butter and as crazy as their owner.

Occasionally a cattle dealer might venture up to buy one and be met either with a torrent of abuse or a brazen denial that there was such a thing as a four-footed beast about the place. The roof of her dwelling was decorated with the skeletons of cats and fowl that had departed this life, but what ritual significance this may have had no one ever dared to enquire.

Just what constructive role this curious pair played in the natural scheme of things would be hard to define, but one thing is certain. Whether they ever realised it or not, they drove Barney Ned to take the pledge.

Barney swore off the drink at the end of a three-day bender as the January snow was thawing, and many a hardened sinner paused in fright as the news became public, for his binges were legendary and frequent. It was his practice to arrive at Connolly's bar with a parcel of steaks which he would hand without a word to the barmaid. He would then buy a bottle or two or three of the best and retire to a position by the fire in the back room. There he would stay for two or three days, leaving his place only to perform essential tasks such as making room for more booze. Apart from the odd snatch of garbled song or an occasional bellow of 'Steak' he made no fuss, departing as abruptly as he came and leaving Connolly richer for his passing.

Barney was a strong man, strong of mind and body, not to mention bank balance, for he was a substantial farmer. He was not given much to flights of fancy or idle conversation. Booze was his simple pleasure, but he invariably conducted his binges in mid-week and never once missed church on Sunday, a pillar of rectitude in his blue suit. Many people wondered how he did it. The more dissolute wondered how his constitution stood the strain and the more puritan wondered how the bank balance held out. Something all sides were agreed on was that something would have to give, but what gave eventually was the most unexpected thing of all and that was Barney's thirst.

It was a Thursday night when Barney rose abruptly from his seat beside Connolly's fire and headed out into the brilliant moonlight and a spell of industrious sobriety. The countryside had been covered with snow at the start of his visit but the thaw had set in thirty-six hours before. A hard frost for two nights had dried and whitened the mountain road and Barney listened with satisfaction to the metallic ring of his boots on the hard road as he headed for the bridge and home. On the bridge he paused, but whether from necessity of nature or to admire the bright-as-day wintry landscape it will never be known, for while he was looking over the parapet he saw something moving along the stony path that skirted the river.

It was Wee John McNally with the inevitable wool-bale on his back. In the bag something was squirming and a shocking realisation dawned on Barney. Wee John was going to drown pups in the pool below the stepping stones and one thing that Barney had been trying to get all year was a pup from McNally's bitch.

'McNally!' roared Barney from the bridge. 'Houl' on! I want wan of them pups!'

Wee John gave a half-look over his shoulder and broke into a shambling run. Barney slithered down the slope at one side of the bridge and took off in pursuit, alternately cursing Wee John and imploring him to stop. John's legs were short and his burden was unco-operative but for a while he managed to keep a respectable distance in front of Barney. Barney, in spite of his three-day sojourn by Connolly's fireside, was fit enough to get within reaching distance of the bag. It was just as he made a grab for it that he realised that the demon drink had finally caught up with him and was about to exact its horrible revenge, for at that precise moment a dog thrust its head out of the bag and spoke to him.

Well, it didn't exactly speak. More precisely, it cursed fluently and at length, referring in minute detail to Barney's dubious ancestry, immediate parentage and present drunken state. It also advised him to do unnatural and physically impossible things with himself. It further offered to get out of the bale and pitch him headlong into the river, which action, the dog swore, would sober him up in a hurry.

At this point Barney turned and fled. He didn't stop until he was back on the bridge, and his last view of McNally was of the little man crossing by the stepping stones and heading up the snow-covered fields on the other side of the valley, still with the writhing sack on his back.

Now if you're coming home from a three-day binge and you encounter a neighbour with a wool-bale full of dog on his back, and the dog addresses you in the tones this one had just used to Barney, you do one of two things. You go straight back to the pub or you swear off the drink. Barney may not have had much imagination but he had enough to realise that the road back to Connolly's would in all likelihood lead to more talking dogs, talking sheep and heaven only knows what other four-footed beasts that would attempt to engage him in conversation in the years ahead. Not that the years ahead would be numerous, judging by this night's experience. Barney turned for home. In his agitated state it never struck him that McNally had not stopped to drown the pups. The fact that the writhing sack was still on the little man's back barely registered at all.

McNally carried the sack all the way home. He had carried it all the way from his mother's house on the other side of the valley. He entered his abode and decanted the sack's occupant, for there was only one, on to the bed. He then lit the lamp and bullied the fire into flame. These household duties completed, he turned to the bale's late occupant and launched into a review of the night's events with a flow of invective that his mother could barely have matched.

At the start of the snowstorm his mother had decided that the well-being of her four bullocks would best be safeguarded by bringing them into the house, a room and kitchen affair with a loft reached by a ladder. The cattle enjoyed the novelty for a while and they roamed freely from room to kitchen, trampling the furniture, what there was of it, breaking delph and eating the hay that Jane had thoughtfully disposed about the place for their refreshment.

At an early stage it became clear that the ground floor was a bit crowded, so armed with some provisions she took refuge in the loft. The cattle, in their amiable blundering about, soon knocked the ladder down and trampled it into matchwood, leaving Jane as firmly marooned as if she had been on a desert island.

It was the second day of thaw before Wee John, carrying the inevitable wool-bale, arrived for a visit, for Jane encouraged no socialisation, even with her nearest and dearest. He was only mildly surprised by the bellowing of cattle from within the dwelling, but he had to jump for his life when he opened the door, for four thirst-crazed bullocks ripped the doorposts out of the walls in their frenzied stampede for water. He waded in through the malodorous wreckage and called out his mother's name. After an interval she peered at him from the entrance to the loft, her hair in a halo of rat's tails round her grimy face and the last crust of her rations clutched in one grubby hand. He looked from her unlovely visage to the evidence of the cattle's residence, and he made a momentous decision.

'Ye're comin' home with me, Ma,' he announced.

And so it was that he was standing in the middle of his own kitchen floor in the yellow lamplight and speaking to the shape on the bed. 'In the name-a-God,' he howled at the ceiling, 'what will Barney Ned think of us at all? Don't the people think we're mad enough as it is? I'm tellin' ye, the next time…are ye listenin' to me, are ye?'

There was no reply from the bed. Jane McNally, the foul-mouthed, unwitting ally of total abstinence, was fast asleep.

Adapted versions of the stories, 'The First Day', 'Rural Mafia' and The Sobering of Barney Ned', have been broadcast on 'Bazaar' on BBC Radio Ulster.